J Mosdell

The Village of Mortimer

And other Poems

J Mosdell

The Village of Mortimer
And other Poems

ISBN/EAN: 9783337401382

Printed in Europe, USA, Canada, Australia, Japan

Cover: Foto ©Andreas Hilbeck / pixelio.de

More available books at **www.hansebooks.com**

THE

VILLAGE OF MORTIMER

AND OTHER POEMS.

BY

J. MOSDELL.

Reading:

PRINTED AT THE "READING OBSERVER" STEAM PRINTING WORKS.

1891.

THE FOLLOWING COLLECTION OF POEMS IS

Respectfully Dedicated

(BY KIND PERMISSION)

TO

THE REV. C. L. CAMERON,

VICAR OF MORTIMER,

BY THE AUTHOR.

PREFACE.

In giving publicity to this little collection of Poems, it is perhaps necessary that some explanatory statement should be made respecting them and their appearance in type.

With regard to the Poems themselves, it may be observed that they are the results of the musings of one whose education was of the most elementary character possible ; indeed, so far as *scholastic* training is concerned, it may be pronounced to have been absolutely *nil*. He began work at the early age of eight years, and beyond the alphabet and acquiring a knowledge of the fact that two and two make four, has no distinct recollection of having learned anything during the few years it was his privilege to attend school. The fact is, owing partly to the harsh system in vogue in the schools at that time, and partly from his having been from his earliest infancy an ardent lover of nature and wild freedom, and strongly objecting to anything like restraint, he ever, particularly when the weather was fine, preferred roaming through the lanes and among the woods, watching the beautiful birds and listening to and ever charmed with their ravishing melodies ; or rolling in the lovely green meadows among the cowslips and butter-cups, and inhaling the delightful fragrance that ever comes (especially when newly rolled or rolled upon) from the beautiful herbage growing amid the young and tender grass ; or paddling in the limpid, cooling stream on a hot summer's day, chasing the tadpoles or catching the minnows in the brook, or hauling up the "crawldabs" (crayfish), and—looking at the sun to see if it was time to return home. It would not have done to go too soon, as that would have suggested a difficulty on his arriving there, should he be interrogated respecting his untimely appearance ; of course, if he happened to be late it did not so much matter, as he had invariably "been kept in."

This playing "truant," however, often got him into sore trouble at home, as somehow or other the matter would occasionally leak out. Some humorous lines, bearing upon this matter, taken from a piece entitled " Recollections of my Boyhood," and written merely for amusement, may not be out of place in this connection. Hoping his readers will not be unduly shocked at their extreme levity the author begs to be allowed to transcribe a few stanzas :—

'Twas while living there in that drowsy old town,
    That first I was pack'd off to school,
To learn A, B, C, and the next letter D,
    While striding the form or the stool.

But all unsuccessful I never learned much,
    The alphabet was I think all,
My letters I learned but I all the rest spurned,
    However the teacher might bawl.

Which he sometimes would do, and not only so,
    But also would chastise me sore,
Which made me but hate both himself and the slate
    And all the book's confounding lore.

In Wokingham 'twas that I first degrees took,
    'Twas there that I first went to school,
To learn wrong from right and my lessons to slight
    And sometimes get stood on the stool.

'Twas thus that I soon won distinction and fame,
    And left my companions behind,
By this means I rose o'er my friends and my foes,
    The triumph of matter o'er mind.

And thus too I soon became known thro' the school,
    Exalted my fellows above,
Who all of them gazed to see me thus raised,
    But gazed more in mischief than love.

Their gaze I returned, I could all of them see,
    Not one from my look was exempt,
Perch'd high on a stool (as if born but to rule),
    I view'd the whole lot with contempt.

The teacher, of course, was attentive to me,
    He could not neglect such a lad,
But took a delight in thus wreaking his spite,
    He seemed to regard me as bad.

One cold frosty morning, I well recollect,
    Arriving at school rather late,
My fingers so cold that I scarcely could hold
    With comfort the book or the slate ;

But this notwithstanding of course I must rise,
    At once in my place I must stand,
And though a mere child somewhat wayward and wild,
    Was order'd to hold out my hand.

The "pointer" he then would let fall with a whack,
    My fingers did tingle with pain,
Then back to my place with a woe-be-gone face,
    At once I was order'd again.

This harsh treatment it was which made me dislike
    The schooling of those early days,
The infliction of pain with pointer or cane
    My strongest resentment would raise.

And hence it would happen that often I roamed
    And strayed far away from the school,
'Neath skies bright and blue where the tall cowslips grew,
    'Twas there that I went as a rule.

Though this I enjoyed and preferr'd it to that,
    My pleasures would end but in pain,
When homewards I went back to school I was sent,
    And stood on the stool once again.

Again to be stared at by all the rude boys,
    Sly young ignoramuses they,
Who turned up their eyes with delightful surprise,
    Respectful attentions to pay.

Like Saul, head and shoulders above them I stood,
    Like him but a king in disguise,
Advanced to a throne, crown and sceptre alone
    Were needed to give me the rise.

Foolscap on my head would have served for a crown,
 The pointer a sceptre had been,
Had I then but these the long robe and the keys,
 A monarch they all might have seen.

There calmly I stood contemplating the boys
 And eyeing the crafty old man,
Who thought *he* was king and myself a mere thing
 Which he at his pleasure might "tan."

A bright looking object the old member was,
 With spectacles straddling his "beak,"
Through which he would look at the slate or the book,
 But *over* them when he would speak.

His pate was as bald as the globe on the stand,
 Resembling a bladder of lard,
Round, chubby and fat, though of course for "a' that"
 The top of his "cranny" was hard.

"A bright shining place where no parting was known,"
 Devoid of all semblance of hair,
Nor wool, fleck, nor down, could be seen on his crown,
 Long since it had ceased to grow there.

But of this enough, or the writer's readers will weary at
the threshold. His father's profession or calling in life was
that of a cordwainer, as will be seen from the poem entitled
"Reminiscences of Home," and having a large family,
mostly boys, and being, of course, but a poor man, it was
perhaps a matter of necessity with him that his sons should
have been early put to the "seat." As, however, the
writer grew older, he became more thoughtful and strove to
cultivate his mind in many ways, and he thinks he is entitled
to say, without any fear of its being attributed to vanity or
egotism on his part, that his verses are evidence that he has
not altogether failed in his attempts at self-culture. Having
thus cleared the ground with regard to himself his more
cultivated readers will, of course, be prepared to make all
due allowance, and not be too captious or over critical, or
unduly harsh in their strictures upon one who, as the foregoing statement clearly shows, can lay no claim whatever to

anything like erudition, or literary and classical scholarship or attainments.

Now concerning their publication. The writer had been in the habit of occasionally sending small scraps of verse to a local paper, and a gentleman (who desires his identity may not be made public) who always read them as they appeared from time to time in the columns of the *Reading Observer*, wrote to their author suggesting the desirability of having "all his poems printed in a volume," as he considered they were well worthy of being preserved. It need not here be mentioned what inducement was offered or what incentive accompanied this kind and gentlemanly suggestion. Suffice it to say that having mentioned the matter privately (with-holding, of course, the name) to one or two well-informed persons with a view to eliciting their opinion in regard to it, and having been congratulated by them in consequence and advised by all means to accede to this kind request and accept this very generous offer, it was decided (after much deliberation in the writer's own mind as well) to allow the greater portion of them to appear.

It is, of course, not thought that this poetry (if poetry it may be called) will in any way supersede what is already in existence by more gifted writers ; or that it will add much in the way of charms to the floods of sweet song, which, in all metres and in all possible styles of composition, have, during the last century in particular, stirred the human heart to its deepest depths, appealing as it does, and as nothing else can, to the emotional nature of mankind. Their com-position has often had the effect of dispersing the dark clouds that have hung over many a cheerless hour, and of lifting the mind of the writer up and away from the dreary monotony and dull routine of business life. When on his homeward journey in the gloom of winter, oppressed with a sense of extreme loneliness and utter isolation, feeling as though cut off from all human sympathy, and deprived of all earthly friendship, the muse has sometimes taken him kindly by the hand and on Pegasean wing he has mounted aloft and been lifted as it were from his fleshly tenement and made to forget for the while his dismal and unhappy surroundings. Indeed, at times so great has been the pleasure derived from his musings, that he has often, for very joy, thanked God for the fact and boon of existence.

He does not, of course, anticipate that any similar feeling of pleasure or exultation will be evoked in the minds of his readers ; but if any sad, lonely and afflicted spirit, pining in secret sorrow and writhing in mental anguish beneath the blighting stroke of bereavement, shall in any way catch their inspiration and be enabled thereby to look up and away from this transitory state of being, to that wherein our physically disembodied friends' continued existence is something more than a grand and glorious possibility, something more than a mere matter of conjecture and belief, to which all would fain cling with most affectionate tenacity, but is indeed and moreover an incontrovertible and well established fact, a fact as susceptible of proof as any other with which we are acquainted, one which can be, and is, testified and sworn to by a vast number of most credible and most reliable witnesses in all parts of the world, and is moreover supported and sustained by an amount of evidence that is simply overwhelming and irresistible.   If any such shall be cheered into fresh hopefulness and made to forget their griefs by a perusal of these pages, his unpretending verses will not have been printed in vain.   That they may serve some such useful purpose is the sincere wish and fervent hope of their humble author,

J. M.

Mortimer, *June, 1891.*

INDEX.

MORTIMER.

THE WOODS.

Dear favoured village, thy native charms I sing !
  (Has no fond bard those charms e'er sung before ?)
I mount aloft on Contemplation's wing,
    And o'er thy hills and dales my muse shall soar,
    Whence I in tuneful verse thy beauties will explore.

Ah, little know mankind the gem thou art,
    Thou has a world of beauty all thine own,
Uniquely excellent is ev'ry part,
    As all can testify, who have thee known
    And rambled thro' thy glades in concert or alone.

The breezes that upon thy Common play,
    Though sometimes keen, yet most salubrious are,
Health-giving odours from the pine trees, they
    Diffuse around and scatter near and far,
    Impregnating the air, like some all-potent star.

Thy pretty Common is a tableland,
    Whence narrow lanes do slope on every side,
Down which the youthful lover, hand in hand,
    With her who hopes some day to be his bride,
    Their devious way oft take with mutual love and pride.

In close proximity the pine trees grow,
    Near neighbours they of whom we all are proud,
And often to their solitudes we go
    When winds are raving angrily and loud,   [bowed,
    And watch them, as they bend as though in prayer they

B

And listen to the sounds they ever make,
    As through their branches the wild winds do roar,
When every twig doth quiver and doth shake
    As though some terror all unfelt before,
      Their trembling limbs had seized amid the forest hoar.

Sometimes they groan as though by pain opprest,
    At times they whistle as by joy impelled,
Anon they shriek with terror all contest,
    As 'tween their lines the madden'd furies yell'd,
      And then again they seem in rapture's transports held.

Sometimes their dismal sound resembles more—
    When wintry winds through all their spaces blow—
The far-off murm'ring on Alaska's shore
    Of hungry wolves, who, moaning as the go,
      Presage their own approach, and thus the danger show.

They all together stand, yet seem alone,
    So much alike, they all appear as one ;
In mournful melody they sigh and moan
    And other company they seem to shun,
      Since trees of other kind amongst them there are none.

They tower aloft, each one is strong and tall,
    Their strength upon their unity depends,
For if they stood alone, each soon would fall,
    Each unto each some kind assistance lends
      And hence perhaps it is they are such constant friends.

Unlike the sturdy oak which never breaks
    And sends its roots deep down into the soil,
The fir tree just the pleasant surface takes,
    Avoiding labour and all useless toil
      Which all life's ease and pleasure would but mar and spoil.

And, oh ! what numbers throng on ev'ry side
    And stretch before us as we onward go ;
Shoulder to shoulder, as in mutual pride,
    A vast unbroken mighty phalanx show
      As armies have been seen when charging on the foe.

Their palm-like tops all closely interlaced,
    Shut out the sun's fierce heat and burning glare,
And 'neath their cooling shadows I have paced
    Enjoying much the quiet stillness there,
    More sacred far to me than any house of prayer.

And, oh ! how picturesque these pine-woods are,
    Both ornamental and most useful too,
Health-giving properties they send afar ;
    Advantage to consumptives might accrue   [view.
    If here they pitched their tents with these grand pines in

And other woods there are in easy reach,
    Where trees of sorts in wild profusion grow ;
The stately elm, the tall and graceful beech,
    The bending ash that greets us as we go
    And unto all alike profound respect doth show.

These woods are beautiful, with hill and dale
    And pleasant uplands stretching far and wide,
Or sloping downwards to the peaceful vale
    Where tiny streamlets ripple as they glide,
    Murm'ring sweetest music as 'neath moss beds they hide.

Slope facing slope, where trees unnumber'd rise
    And look like two menacing armies there ;
Branches like weapons pointing to the skies,
    As they in deadly conflict would prepare
    When thro' their spaces now the sunlight sends a glare,

And all at once their branches flash and gleam,
    Like spears and swords they glitter overhead,
And for the moment these like those do seem ;
    The woods in places are all flaming red
    And battle seems begun, though by no leader led.

And so indeed it has, for round us fall,
    O'ercome and beaten in the conflict there,
Unnumber'd heroes, who, both great and small,
    Life's transient honours did once proudly bear,
    As flutt'ring in the breeze they look'd so young and fair.

B 2

Ah, yes it has, for autumn now is here,
 And at his coming many leaves turn red,
Some sickly pale and others brown and sere ;
 Then, by the living sap no longer fed,
 Drop from the parent stem and mingle with the dead.

There, all unheeded and unburied, lie
 The leaves that once those branches did adorn
Until October's winds came rushing by,
 When from their places they were rudely torn
 And scatter'd here and there and thro' the forest borne.

And thoughtlessly we now upon them tread
 Forgetting once how beautiful they were,
When, sparkling on the branches overhead,
 Flutt'ring and dancing in the sunlight there
 When gentle breezes sway'd the palpitating air.

But there they lie and rot, and one might think
 That now no int'rest in the tree they took,
As all unsightly from our gaze they shrink
 And more repulsive than attractive look.
 Disfigured, soiled and stained, like some ill-uséd book.

But nature will no idleness allow,
 And e'en these leaves, although they now are dead,
Back to the parent tree ungrudging now
 Must give the substance with which they were fed,
 And help sustain the tree whose roots beneath are spread.

For moisten'd by the rains which now succeed,
 They mingle with the mire and decompose ;
And thus the roots with nourishment they feed
 As downwards thus it percolates and flows ;
 'Tis thus the tree is fed, expands and thrives and grows.

And thus, though dead, they seem again to live,
 As through the tree fresh energy they send ;
Rich, vitalizing properties they give,
 Which from the roots all up the trunk ascend
 And with each branch and twig at once unite and blend.

Then from the ends there shortly shoot and grow
  A fresh supply exactly like the last,
So near the likeness is, 'twould seem as though
    They were the same that from the trees were cast
    When thro' the forest went the gentle autumn blast.

Yes, there is war, although the forces there
  Instead of being centred are withdrawn ;
And very soon the trees will all be bare,
    The sap will from their twig-ends all be gone
    And they all naked stand awaiting spring's glad dawn.

The battle then that there is being waged
  Is purely negative ; no hostile force
In sanguinary conflict there engaged,
    No warrior charging on his war-trained horse ;
    The battle, after all, is nature's peaceful course.

Then oh ! what lovely, secret walks abound,
  What pleasant bye-paths here and there we find,
Where one can walk and catch each rural sound
    With more distinctness to the ear and mind,
    As leisurely we go, to musing still inclined.

The silence there at intervals is sweet,
  At intervals 'tis broken by a song
Which pleasantly the list'ning ear doth greet,
    In sweetest cadence merrily and long
    Its notes are clear and shrill, its vocal powers are strong.

And now the jay's strange voice is loudly heard—
  A wild harsh note that through the woodland rings—
Contrasting strongly with each other bird,
    As through the woods its screeching notes it flings
    And in the distance now it flaps its light brown wings.

Oh ! how delightful in these lovely glades
  To pause and listen as we onward go
Beneath the tall trees' cooling pleasant shades,
    When summer's burning heats upon us glow   [throw.
    As they their long arms stretch and wide their shadows

To pause and listen to the sounds that break
　At intervals upon the ravished ear,
As through the quiet woods our way we take,
　When nought that could disturb our minds is near,
　And nature smiles around and all the skies are clear.

To listen to the sounds that ever come
　From nature's temple, where the wild birds dwell,
Whose cheerful voices with the insects' hum
　Upon each passing breeze ascend and swell,
　Bewitching all the woods with their resistless spell.

And now the magpie, screaming as it flies,
　Flaps its broad wings and spreads its ample tail,
As yonder in the distance there he hies
　With her whose love for him can never fail,　　　[wail.
　Though storms around them rave and wintry winds may

Now overhead I hear a gentle noise
　And then a sound as though something had fell,
And looking up a squirrel there enjoys
　A nut, which he has cracked and dropt the shell,
　Which his judicious choice will there explain and tell.

Upon his haunches there the creature sits,
　His little optics glaring down on me,
And if I chance to move, at once he quits
　His hold ; and, bounding higher up the tree,
　Thence cunningly looks back—a saucy fellow he.

And now throughout each silent glade and glen,
　A cry resounds, both sudden, sharp and clear,
Which echo's answering voice repeats again
　In faint replies, borne back upon the ear
　With feeble indistinctness sounding far and near.

The woodcock 'tis, whose mellow flute-like notes
　Reverberate through all the spaces there ;
To rapid time its charming music floats,
　So rich in volume, 'tis unique and rare,
　Its tenor is supreme amid the concert fair.

The woods are redolent with music sweet,
   Bird answers bird till echo faint replies;
Harmonious sounds the raptured senses greet,
   In charming modulations, fall and rise,
     Till those sweet songsters cease, when all the music dies.

Oh ! how I love these woods to ramble through,
   Beneath the shelter of the friendly trees,
When scalding rays that stream from yonder blue
   Are mildly temper'd with a gentle breeze,
     And ev'rything brings joy that one's glad vision sees.

How oft when strolling 'neath their grateful shade
   When summer's heat the o'ergrown grass has dried,
And list'ning to each sound the winds have made
   As through the rustling fern-leaves at my side
     Some presence all unseen around me seem'd to glide.

How often have I halted there to gaze
   In rapture on the scene around me spread ;
The arching blue with sunlight all ablaze,
   The graceful branches waving o'er my head
     And beauty ev'rywhere attend each step I tread.

There have I stood in silence and alone,
   A strange delight possessing all my frame ;
And, as by instinct, to the Great Unknown
   My thoughts have turned, to Whose life-breathing flame
     All things existence owe, and all fair things first came.

'Tis sweet to ramble through these silent glades
   When morning's all-inspiring breath exhales,
Or when the peaceful day declines and fades
   And twilight through their fastnesses prevails,
     Though *then* a sense of dread the timid heart assails.

The birds whose notes so merrily had rung
   All through the day now hide their heads in sleep,
And silent is each music-making tongue,
   As over all night's gloom begins to creep
     And darkness ev'rywhere falls on the wooded deep.

Then strange weird sounds from out their vastness come,
  Mysterious whispers there sometimes are heard,
As through some hollow trunk the night winds hum ;
  Or fearful shriek from that gloom-loving bird
  The owl, whom something now has startled and disturbed.

And now, perhaps, a rabbit has been caught
  And held a pris'ner in the well-set snare,
Which some unkind, harsh nature there had brought
  And covered over with much thought and care
  With rubbish and dry leaves that it had gather'd there.

And all at once there break upon the ear
  The cry of anguish and the shriek of pain,
And timid natures, shudder, shrink and fear,
  As through the woods the cry resounds again
  And still reverberates in echo's sad refrain.

And now the winds again begin to moan
  And make queer noises in the trees around ;
At times they sigh, anon they creak and groan
  Straining one's nerves with their most dismal sound
  Suggesting ugly thoughts at ev'ry rising mound.

Sounds heard at night bring terror to the mind,
  That scarcely would be noticed in the day,
And in the darkness nervous natures find
  Their superstitious fancies freely play
  Which if not held in check soon lead them far astray.

By day or night all through the changing year,
  These solemn woods most interesting seem,
Their sombre presence when night's shades appear,
  Or cheering aspect in the morning's beam,
  And at all other times their charms appear supreme.

When spring returns in beauty all arrayed
  And birds awake from their long winter sleep,
When odours from the violet scent the glade
  And ev'rywhere the primroses now peep
  Up the ascending slope and down the craggy steep.

Then through the woods activity is rife
  And all around the buds begin to show ;
On ev'ry hand are signs of busy life,
  As once again the sap begins to flow
  Now that the frost is gone and melted is the snow.

The tender bud is all that yet is seen,
  'Tis but the promise of what soon will be,
When over all a robe of richest green
  Not from without, but from within, we see
  By evolution thrown on ev'ry spreading tree.

O ! what a picture then these woods present !
  What wealth of beauty stretching ev'rywhere,
All by the gracious kind Creator lent
  To give us pleasure and relieve our care ;
  He surely must be good who made the woods thus fair.

When through these latitudes the lord of day
  Rides grandly in his all-victorious car,
The woods responsive own his potent sway
  As o'er each hill and dale he flings afar
  His radiant beams; his trophies earth's green garlands are.

In "leafy June," in August and July,
  These woods are simply heaven upon earth,
The trees are in their prime and cannot die,
  Wild flowers are springing into lovely birth,
  The birds all jubilant ; it is their time of mirth.

And in the autumn ; O ! what beauty then,
  Eclipsing all the glories of the spring
When but *one* colour stretched through glade and glen
  (As but one song the thrush is known to sing)
  All colours now combine and fresh attractions bring.

A halo round each dying leaf is cast,
  A beauty lingers on each fading tree,
Prismatic hues on all the woods set fast ;
  No sight more lovely than this scene could be
  Which nature spreads around most lavishly and free.

'Tis life in death, that which we now behold,
  'Tis beauty blossoming amid decay,
'Tis wealth's profusion in a blaze of gold,
  'Tis nature's fancy in most active play,
    Adorning ev'ry sprig as for some festal day.

If this is death, then death most lovely is,
  And of its presence none need be afraid ;
'Tis but the prelude to substantial bliss
  To which we pass by its most friendly aid.
    We should no terror feel, we should not be dismayed.

The spring, the summer, and the autumn too,
  Each has a charm peculiarly its own ;
The face of nature, spring's glad beams renew,
  In summer's heat all to perfection grown,
    And in the autumn tints the grandest sights are shown.

And in the winter, with their arms all bare,
  When one might think no beauty could be seen,
That nought but gloom and dreariness were there,
  Where just before such loveliness had been,   [green ;
    When all the woods were deck'd with various shades of

Yes, even then, when mists and fogs prevail,
  And chilling vapours fill each glade and glen,
Or plaintively the winds sob, sigh and wail
  O'er ev'ry hillock and each swampy fen
    And pine in discontent thro' all their spaces then.

Yes even then I oft have noted well
  The fascinating charms which they possess,
Inherent qualities that cast a spell
  O'er every contemplative mind, no less
    Than when they were arrayed in summer's richest dress.

Who that has seen these woods can e'er forget
  The gay appearance they at times present,
When all their twigs and branches, dripping wet,
  And earthwards their long stretching arms are bent
    Exhausted and o'ercome, their energies all spent.

When through the open cloud-rift all askance
  A ray of sunlight flashes quickly there,
The eye beholds with one enraptured glance
    Unnumbered diamonds glitt'ring in the air.
    All sparkling in the light and glinting everywhere.

Or when the frost, that wonder-working thing,
  Its tracery so delicately hangs
Upon the webs that from the branches swing,
    So neatly woven with the spiders' fangs   [pangs.
    Where doubtless not long since the flies endured death's

And on the trees, each branch and tiny twig,
  As on the grass each spiral glitt'ring blade,
Upon each trembling spray and quiv'ring sprig :
    On all alike its drapery is laid
    And all looks lovely there in purest white arrayed.

Indeed no sight could well delight us more
  Than this grand presence which we now behold.
Transforming every object with its hoar
    (As did the autumn with its tints of gold)
    As all it doth embrace and everything enfold.

What fairies in these woods have been at work !
  What unseen artists have been sketching there !
Revealing beauties that around us lurk,
    All unsuspected in the viewless air.
    Portraying them on trees with matchless skill and care !

Their work is quickly and most nobly done,
  With faultless taste and most consummate skill ;
Than gleam of stars they other light had none
    To lend them aid, as they their tasks fulfil :
    The magic must be wrought solely by strength of will.

'Tis beautiful and will inspection bear,
  The more 'tis seen, the more we do admire ;
The trees a saint-like, heavenly aspect wear,
    So calm and still, as upwards they aspire,
    Suggesting thoughts of peace which human hearts desire.

"Twill thus be seen the woods can hold their own
　E'en in the winter, as when spring is here,
That then they have their charms, as I have shown,
　That then, at times, most lovely they appear
　Although their leaf is gone and they are brown and sere.

And now farewell ye lovely glades and glens!
　I've lingered long enjoying much your charms.
Adieu! ye sloping vales and marshy fens,
　Ye tow'ring trees with long extended arms,
　Nocturnal terrors and your baseless false alarms.

SOCIAL ASPECTS, TRADES, &c.

O! Mortimer! most privileged art thou!
　Not for thy woods alone, though they are grand :
Nor for thy lofty common's tow'ring brow,
　By healthful breezes regularly fann'd,
　And none more picturesque in this delightful land.

Nor for thy famous waving pines alone,
　Whose turpentiny properties impart
Enduring benefits, as have been shown,
　Unto the sinking and despairing heart,
　Causing fresh hope to spring and bidding fears depart.

But that thy people have within their reach
　All means of self-improvement at command ;
Respected leaders too have we who teach
　What they themselves most clearly understand,　[plann'd.
　How this huge globe was framed and for man's comfort

We have our churches and our chapels too,
  (We have alas! the public house as well)
Our evening classes where the wiser few
    Seek fellowship; their thoughts exchange and tell,
    Church Guild and Meeting-room and Temperance Hotel.

We have our concerts, and we lectures hear,
  Have entertainments which we much enjoy,
And village minstrels, promenading near,
    Whose music doth all quietude destroy—
    A band of beardless youths led by some gifted boy.

All kinds of shops and "ready money stores,"
  And many trades are represented here,
Over the "last" the good cordwainer pores
    From morn till night, all through the changing year,
    His bristles, wax and tools, all close at hand and near.

The harness-maker, with his many boys,
  All healthy, saucy, and all fat and strong;
Who as they each grow up their dad employs;
    All short and thick although their name is "Long,"
    In saying which I mean no disrespect or wrong.

We have the blacksmith, whose strong brawny arms
  The pond'rous hammer can most freely swing,
Whose heavy thuds, commingling with the charms
    Of smaller hammer, do resound and ring,
    As they the heated iron to shape and beauty bring.

Whose roaring bellows and whose flaming forge
  Have their attractions for the young and fair,
Who love to see the glitt'ring sparks disgorge
    From out the chimney on the dark'ning air,
    And flutter, dance and fly until they perish there.

We have the "carpenter and builder" too,
  Two trades distinct, but here in one combined,
Either or both he undertakes to do
    With satisfaction to each heart and mind;
    Most practical is he, to business much inclined.

One good "machinist," who well understands
   In all its details his most useful trade,
With skilful brain and ever busy hands
   Untiringly he labours ; not afraid
   Of honest toil, by which his living must be made.

We have the "Sanitary Engineer,"
   Who in himself doth quite a host combine,
Since "painter, plumber," both in him appear,
   Fitting and paperhanging, all his line,
   "Glazier and decorator," this namesake of mine.

Bricklayers, wheelwrights, and one noble sweep,
   One trav'lling tinker, with an ass and cart,
Who travels far and wide that he may reap
   The fruits of industry ; his humble part
   Is mending pots and pans, no novice in his art.

Black diamond merchants, one, two, three and four,
   Whose wares do glisten as they pass along,
Profusely they their glitt'ring wealth outpour
   When winter reigns and frosts are keen and strong,
   When nights are dark and cold and winds rave loud and
      long.

We have a brewery, where beer is made,
   "Good beer" no doubt 'tis, as the saying goes,
Its head is a consistent man of trade,
   And all his energy into it throws ;
   He is a Christian, too, as all the village knows.

A blind "mat-maker," who, though sight is gone,
   The sense of touch retaineth most acute,
Although to him the morning has no dawn,
   And he less gifted than the humble brute,
   Yet doth he not complain, nor with high heaven dispute.

All through the week he toileth at his trade,
   And on Lord's day at Church is ever seen
Among the choir in snow-like robe arrayed,
   With calm expression and a saint-like mien,
   His *inner* sight is strong, his mental vision keen.

We have a kiln, where bricks are burnt and made
  Of clay, an inexhaustible supply
Of finest texture to the sight display'd ;
    A large, huge mound that slopes up to the sky,   [eye.
    From which the more they take, the more yet greets the

Bricks, tiles and pipes in order there arranged,
  All picturesque and looking brightly red,
The clay's brown nature has to redness changed
    Since it was taken from its earthy bed,
    And heated in the flames by fuel so freely fed.

And then the last, though by no means the least,
  That I would mention, ere this branch I quit,
And turn my thoughts once more unto the east,
    ('Tis to the west my fancy now doth flit)   [lit.
    From whence the wise men came by strangest light then

We have a firm who, not unknown to fame,
  A useful industry that doth employ
Both man and beast : with lathe and bending frame
    Unevenness and crookedness destroy,
    In rough and twisted stakes brought there by carter boy.

They steam them well until they are quite wet,
  Then " frame " them 'neath a heavy hanging weight,
To proper shape they thus these rude poles get,
    They yield and give until they are quite straight,
    Then all are soundly dried and for the lathe they wait,

In which their further imperfections fly,
  Pimples and blotches all soon disappear,
Till, round and smooth, fine "handles" greet the eye ;
    Their surfaces all polish'd white and clear,
    As banded round with withes in bundles lying near.

Then carted off and to the rail conveyed,
  Their distant destinations soon they reach,
To "order" they are sent as unto "order" made ;
    Reliable and strong, collectively and each,
    All made of pliant ash, or more unbending beech.

To noblest uses then these "sticks" are put,
  Or rather "handles" (that is now their name),
They once were "sticks" when growing from the root,
  And ere they had been straighten'd by the frame,
  Or in the lathe been turn'd, whence they in "handles" came.

No broom without a handle is complete,
  Nor can the prong be used without its aid ;
When 'mid the new-mown grass's fragrance sweet
  'Tis toss'd and turn'd until the hay is made,
  When 'tis all carted thence and to the rick convey'd.

Blind-rollers also (for they cannot see),
  And crutches, too, which are both straight and strong ;
Mop-handles, stool-legs, either four or three,
  Tub-rests and peel-sticks, lanky, thin and long,
  And other uses, too, unmentioned in my song.

And rakes by thousands also here are made,
  Hay-making rakes, their teeth all made of wood,
With bands of tin and wire are firmly stay'd
  And held together in a working mood,
  They satisfaction give as 'tis well meant they should.

Rat-catcher and dog-trainer, too, have we,
  Whose dogs together frolic, frisk and play ;
Obnoxious rats' stern foe in one we see,
  As with his ferrets he doth on them prey,
  Or slaying them outright, or driving them away.

Cab-men and fly-men from their places run,
  And carriers' vans may here be daily seen ;
(The latter class are somewhat overdone).
  Sports oft take place, an animating scene,
  And cricket matches play'd upon the "village green."

Our sisters, too, much talent do display,
  Excelling much in their respective spheres ;
Dressmakers, artists and wool-workers they,
  (Most fit companions for their male compeers),
  And famous laundresses, and music's forte appears.

Here comely ladies have their dresses made,
 Which fit them well and their good figure show ;
With much artistic skill in them display'd,
  Each wearer's beauty seems the more to grow,
  As round each pretty form resistless charms they throw.

Wools of all colours and unnumber'd shades,
 By clever fingers are most deftly wrought
To all designs : branches, leaves, flowers and blades
  Of waving grass, which show much skill and thought.
  Moving admiration and praises all unsought.

Clothes washed and dried until they look like snow,
 Starch'd, iron'd and glazed until with light they shine,
And faultless, absolute perfection show ;
  Their polish'd surfaces so superfine
  Add lustre to their wearers, tradesman or divine.

The brush, or crayon, they with skill can use
 And pretty pictures on the canvas throw,
Depicting scenes in captivating hues
  And much artistic genius they show,
  Their powers are manifold as we are proud to know.

The soft piano, or the sweet guitar,
 The concertina, or the violin,
They can manipulate ; and sweeter far
  Doth seem their music and its way doth win
  Deep down into the heart, stirring the soul within.

Our homes they brighten and our lives they cheer,
 Our joys partake and all our sorrows share,
Express their sympathy in falling tear,
  Speak words of comfort to relieve our care,
  And by the power of love our burdens help to bear.

Here city tradesmen have their country seat,
 And independent clergymen are here,
Who in their wisdom chose this grand retreat
  With hills and dales and charming woods so near,
  And interesting walks that all around appear.

  C

And round about us titled people dwell,
 The aristocracy have mansions near ;
True noblemen in name and deeds as well,
 True ladies also at their sides appear,
 M.P.'s and Baronets, a goodly sample here.

Their presence lends *eclat* unto the place,
 To village life a dignity imparts ;
We note their manners and we scan their face,
 And try to look deep down into their hearts,
 If we can there discern false simulation's arts,

Or human sympathy and Christian love
 Towards their brethren who are poor and low,
Which " like some Angel from the realms above "
 Shall visit them when in the depths of woe,
 And brighten up their lives and heavenly comfort show.

These latter feelings their kind natures sway,
 And in their hearts the former have no place.
Their poorer brethren oft and frequent they
 Both visit and encourage ; their kind face
 An inspiration is, to those in sorrow's case.

I oft have noted Christian ladies go
 To some poor neighbour who was sick and ill,
Their love and sympathy with him to show,
 And thus their mission upon earth fulfil,
 And minister to him with cheerful mind and will.

The little basket borne upon the arm
 Containing something for the sick man's room,
His failing appetite to tempt and charm ;
 The kindly word that shall disperse his gloom,   [fume.
 And leave a fragrance there like some sweet flower's per-

Sisters of mercy, angels in disguise,
 Who walk the earth in garb of human clay,
Attracting earth-bound mortals to the skies,
 Whither themselves would seem to lead the way,
 Its light already streams and round them seems to play.

CHARITIES, PUBLIC AND PRIVATE SCHOOLS, AND THE VICARAGE INSTITUTE.

We have our charities and public schools,
  Where youthful talent is developed fast,
Where discipline maintains her wholesome rules ;
  The master's watchful eye o'er all is cast,
  And each child's progress he desires from first to last.

And private schools : one noble Institute,
  Of which the Vicar is the worthy head,
Where first the mind in learning's soil takes root,
  By gifted tutors studiously led ;
  With wholesome mental food each craving mind is fed.

There, sons of noblemen first lessons take,
  There, life's foundations are most firmly laid,
There, first the light on their young minds doth break,
  There, first impressions are received and made,
  And there success ensured in learning's every grade.

And who can tell what those dear boys shall be
  In after years, when older heads are grey,
When from the school and all restraints set free
  Out in the world they push their hopeful way ?
  God grant they may do well, and none e'er go astray.

Who knows, but that among that youthful throng
  Some giant intellect may slumber there,
Some mighty master of the art of song,
  Who shall to nations yet unborn declare
  In charms of matchless verse the secrets of the air.

C 2

Some gifted Sculptor, who shall bring to view
   The charms that now lie hidden in the stone,
As chip by chip, with skill and patience too,
   He labours on untiring and alone
    Till to admiring crowds his angel he has shown.

Some great Inventor or some Engineer,
   Whose wondrous works the world shall yet surprise ;
Some Prophet-genius, or gifted Seer,
   Whose hand shall draw the curtain from the skies,
    Revealing to mankind what in the future lies.

Some rising Barrister who holds a brief
   (And holds his learnèd audience as well),
His flowing eloquence finds glad relief,
   Wrapping his hearers in magnetic spell,
    As he his client's cause in moving speech doth tell.

Some great Astronomer, who shall survey
   The boundless spaces that around us are,
Pursue the comet through yon " milky way,"
   Old Saturn's brilliant rings describe afar
    Nebulæ analyze and name each distant star.

Some fluent Orator, who through the land
   Shall pour his eloquence, a silver tide,
While list'ning multitudes shall round him stand,
   Applaud each sentence with becoming pride,
    His perorations hear, his fame spread far and wide.

Some polished Statesman, who his country's cause
   Shall ever plead in accents firm and clear,
And help to frame still yet more perfect laws
   Than those which on the statute book appear,
    And through all troubled seas the State-ship help to steer.

Some brilliant Officer, whose genius shall
   O'er England's forces make his name supreme,
And at his bidding surging hosts shall swell,
   As they of battle's honours proudly dream,
    The martial spirit lead and glory be their theme.

Some keen Philosopher, who shall explore
    The realms of nature and its charms reveal,
And on the page of scientific lore
    Record impressions he himself must feel,
    As to his candid mind his facts with force appeal.

Some Navigator, who through trackless seas
    The vessel's course unerringly shall guide,
As on the boiling surf with graceful ease
    And noble carriage she doth grandly ride,
    Modest in demeanour, with just a show of pride.

Some wise Physician, who shall yet make known
    What he himself by study shall obtain,
To suffering multitudes in every zone
    The grand announcement of a cure for pain,
    Which shall restore the sick to health and strength again.

Some grand Composer who shall sing and soar,
    And from the skies celestial music bring,
In matchless strains his genius outpour,
    O'er all mankind his thrilling raptures fling,
    With which succeeding ages shall resound and ring.

Some sweet Musician, who the sounding lyre
    With skilful fingers shall most nimbly sweep,
Or all-accomplished shall the well-trained choir
    To perfect time and faultless order keep,
    Till 'neath their melting strains the sensitive shall weep.

Some famous Artist, who shall then portray,
    And on the glowing stretch'd-out canvas set
Scenes that for beauty and life-like display
    Shall then eclipse all efforts that way yet,
    And Raphael be dethroned by what we then shall get.

Some stirring Actor who shall grace the stage,
    Uplifting Tragedy and freeing Play
From misconceptions of this canting age,
    Which fears that Passion will lead minds astray,
    And Vice reign over all with undisputed sway.

Some graphic Writer, who with facile pen
  The rising race shall captivate and charm,
Upon all topics shall instruct them then,
    Point out the dangers that around them swarm,
    And how they may avoid contamination's harm.

Some bold Historian, who shall record
  The facts relating to each by-gone age,
How nations in dispute did whet their sword,
    And soon in fearful conflict all engage,
    While shot and deadly shell around them burst and rage.

But that at last a better day has come,
  That trade and commerce flourish everywhere,
And that no longer to the stirring drum,
    Whose tones disturb and agitate the air,
    Mankind for useless strife assemble and prepare.

Some famed Geologist, to whom the earth
  Her hidden secrets shall reveal and show ;
And interesting truths of priceless worth
    Be yet discovered, by which we may know
    Much that relates to man and all this life below.

Some Antiquary who all ancient things
  Which by research he shall explore and find,
That once belonged to peasants or to Kings,
    The rudely vulgar or the more refined,
    Or e'n the most degraded of all human kind.

All these with patience and with skilful care
  He will arrange without a thought of fame,
And with each other broken parts compare,
    Then re-unite them and give each a name,
    Tell what their uses were, and whence each relic came.

Some clever Critic, who shall analyze
  The writings of his fellows ; chiefly those
Who lead the public mind, to whom all eyes
    In controversy turn ; through them he goes,
    Each foible he notes and every error shows.

No foe to learning, he is learning's friend,
  Safe-guarding knowledge and preserving youth,
His efforts in this one direction tend,
    Although at times his manner seems uncouth
    His one sole object is to serve the cause of truth.

Some kind Philanthropist, who shall devote
  All willing powers of body, mind and soul
To one grand cause ; and Howard-like, who wrote
    Indelibly his name on Time's long scroll,
    Humanity's strong claims make life's sole aim and goal.

Some great " Q.C.," who with forensic skill,
  His mind well versed in learning's legal lore,
His spell-bound hearers shall both sway and thrill
    With moving pathos, as he shall outpour
    In floods of eloquence his mind's exhaustless store.

His vast ability all classes then,
  Both Judge and Jury and each Bencher too,
The lower strata and the " upper ten,"
    Societies' ascending grades all through
    Shall much admire and praise and render him his **due**.

Some complicated and perplexing case
  He shall unravel with consummate skill,
His facts arrange in order and in place,
    Light up his periods with his wit until
    His audience laugh or weep at his all-potent will.

Each argument by evidence sustained
  The Gordian knot around the prisoner draws,
Who pale and trembling at the bar arraigned,
    For some infringement of his country's laws,
    Acquitted or condemned amidst suppress'd applause.

Some noted Traveller like Mungo Park,
  Or grand old Livingstone, whose heart of hearts
Yearn'd to his brethren who were black and dark,
    Inside and out in all their many parts, .
    As they in bondage groan'd beneath oppression's smarts.

Some able Hypnotist, whose strength of will
    Shall weaker minds o'ershadow and control,
Entrancing them by his mysterious skill,
    And drawing them as magnets to the pole,
    Until he can " suggest " his purpose to the soul.

By simple passes from his practised hand
    His " subject " he o'erpowers and puts to sleep ;
By some strange power which he doth understand,
    In slumber's depths he doth their senses steep,
    And at his bidding they in perfect stillness keep.

Then skilfully and with much gentle care
    Some malformation with the knife removes,
Which by some freak of nature had grown there,
    And to the rule but the exception proves,
    Since nature seldom leaves her long-accustomed grooves.

The swelling cyst which 'neath the skin had grown,
    A movable and gristly substance there,
Which had at times uneasy symptoms shown,
    Inducing thus much anxious thought and care,
    As still it swelled and grew unto proportions rare.

The painful tooth set firm within the jaw,
    The upper part corroded with decay,
The quiv'ring nerve thus all exposed and raw
    Did writhe in pain and on the system prey   [day.
    All through each sleepless night and through each weary

The splinter'd bone which from the sight concealed,
    Its painful way did work beneath the skin,
And much discomfort thus at times did yield
    As still progressing it its way did win,
    The pain resembling much the prick of some sharp pin.

The ugly tumour that did grow and thrive
    Within the system, unsuspected there,
Absorbing much that kept it well alive,
    Since all life's juices it did draw and share,
    Its own development its constant aim and care.

All these the hypnotist can exorcise,
  Eradicate, remove, or cut away ;
Pain hides its head or at his bidding flies
  As night's grim shadows at the dawn of day
  Flap their dark raven wings before each rising ray.

Some noble Banker, whose financial skill
  And stirling character shall lead the way,
With high endeavour and persistent will
  The sure foundations of his system lay,
  Which shall in future times the money market sway.

His genius shall over all preside,
  In each department and each office there,
With much discernment and much lawful pride,
  Inspecting all accounts with cautious care,
  And auditing the books with unassuming air.

In all transactions with his fellow-men,
  As with each officer who serves within,
His mind's acumen and far-reaching ken
  And courteous treatment their respect shall win,
  His choice urbanity shall first at home begin.

O'er all his huge collossal enterprise
  Wise supervision he will ever keep,
Preventing thus reversion's sad surprise,
  Which oft o'ertakes the men who nod and sleep,
  As they each stupid sense in dull oblivion steep.

When, prices low, the markets are depress'd,
  And trade and commerce pine in discontent,
When all around are signs of much unrest,
  Shares all discounted, and their stocks all spent,
  Transferred to other hands by being sold or lent.

When leading firms reach out and speculate,
  And pledge their credit to undue extent,
When prices fail and markets fluctuate,
  And dividends are not what they were meant,
  Till cash in hand is gone and home resources spent.

When some grave crisis threatens and impends,
　And heedless panic leads the public mind,
When confidence distrusts its long-tried friends ;
　　For being heedless—panic must be blind,
　　And therefore all unfit to mix with human kind.

Resources fail and institutions, all
　Feel more or less the ever-tightening strain,
Banks are besieged and menace their own fall,
　　Unable long such pressure to sustain
　　As that which surges round with still increasing gain.

One firm remains amid the tumult there,
　And all demands can meet and satisfy,
Until the crisis, with its anxious care,
　　Has disappeared from the commercial sky,
　　As cloudlets oft are driven when the winds are high.

Grand possibilities before them lie,
　All these respectively each boy may be,
Their fame spread out beneath the stretching sky,
　　To distant lands beyond the mighty sea,
　　How England's noble sons had blessed humanity.

THE DOCTOR (G.H.D.).

We have a Doctor, whom I had o'erlook'd,
　Whose kind forgiveness I must therefore crave,
My subject's heads I should have ranged and book'd
　　In order ; and this one omission grave
　　My pages had not marr'd ; *his* claims I may not waive.

A kindly, genial, patient man is he.
  With just a vein of humour in his make,
Which sometimes finds expression, when we see
    Fun in his eyes—note the expressive shake
    Of his well-balanced head ; his pun admire and take,

With much appreciation of the wit
  That sometimes flashes from his fertile brain,
When in his surgery we stand or sit,
    Where circumstances us awhile detain,
    As waiting for the draught that shall relieve some pain.

His many patients come from far and near
  For med'cines for themselves or for their friends,
To all he lends a most attentive ear,
    Gives his advice, and consolation sends
    To him who lies at home on whom the bread depends.

His life is one of unremitting toil
  From morn till eve, all through the busy week,
Duties' exactions do the hours despoil,
    In which sweet fellowship he fain would seek
    With those who share his home and his life's pleasures eke.

No time has he that he can call his own,
  In which he can be sure of ease and rest,
Of being undisturb'd and left alone
    With those whose company he loves the best,
    His daughters, wife and sons, with sacred freedom blest.

Not e'en at night, when others soundly sleep,
  Can he be sure of undisturbed repose,
When for a while his senses he would steep
    In sweet oblivion ; sometimes there are those
    Who seek his skilful aid in pain's distracting throes.

And sometimes from long distances they come,
  When nights are bitter with the frost and snow,
When rains are pouring and the wild winds hum,
    When moon nor stars their friendly radiance throw
    'Tis then they often come, imploring him to go

With them to someone who is racked with pain,
  Some sudden illness that has fallen there ;
Some mother's labour that doth sorely strain
  Her weak resources and her strength outwear,
  Whose critical condition needs most skilful care.

Without complaint he rises in the night,
  Responding nobly to the cry of pain,
His patients' lives are precious in his sight,
  None ever cry or call to him in vain,
  With much devotion he bids them their fears restrain.

Oh ! tell me not of those who take their life,
  And hold it loosely in their country's cause,
And who amid stern war's relentless strife,
  Seek glory, honour, and the world's applause
  As they destruction court from cannons' flaming jaws ;

Who to the sound of spirit-stirring drum,
  Or skirling bagpipe or the clarionet,
In order march to where their foemen come
  By music led, their nerves by impulse set,
  Until in deadly strife and fearful conflict met.

True heroes they, and much they do deserve
  Of recognition from their fellow-men,
As from their duties they ne'er shrink or swerve,
  But with true courage rush to action, when
  Their country is imperilled ; serving nobly then.

But here is one who in a better way
  Doth serve humanity ; and greater claims
Has he upon our gratitude, than they
  Who 'mid the roaring cannons' belching flames
  Stand firmly to their guns and win immortal names.

One who, although unknown to sounding fame,
  Unostentatiously pursues his way,
Quiet and unassuming puts to shame
  Those who their gaudy trappings would display,
  Since precious life he saves, which these destroy and slay.

What risks to his own useful life he runs,
  From cold and damp when on his daily calls,
Attending patients—mothers, daughters, sons,
  The young, or aged, on whose head there falls
  The bending weight of years, and pain or weakness galls.

And greater still the danger he incurs,
  When called from home on wild and stormy nights,
When although wrapped in rugs and hairy furs
  The piercing wind most pitilessly bites ;
  And moon nor stars appear with their inspiring lights.

True heroism here is surely seen,
  Or nowhere else can such a thing be found,
If 'tis not *here* it never yet has been,
  And cannot grow in such a barren ground
  As this poor earthly soil, where life's rank weeds abound.

Unchronicled, unhonoured and unsung
  His services unto his country are,
While through the nation's lengths and breadths have rung
  Undying peans sounding near and far,
  In honour of the men who waged successful war.

One humble poet will his praises sing,
  One lowly bard his merits will declare,
Will weave a garland and fresh laurels bring
  With which to crown him, and which he will wear
  With noble dignity and unassuming air.

THE CHURCHES.

We have two Churches, both the gift of one
  Who, though he does not in the place reside,
Is yet a neighbour who hath earned and won
  Our gratitude ; we think of him with pride
  Whose all-embracing heart did for our wants provide.

Vast wealth has he, which wisely he employs
  In building Churches for the people's use,
Where they, in their most sacred solemn joys,
  Their souls' affections from the world set loose, [profuse.
  On faith's strong wings shall soar 'mid heavenly strains

There tott'ring age and youthful vigour meet,
  And men and women in life's golden prime,
And little children's tiny patt'ring feet
  Sound through their tile-paved aisles ; Oh ! 'tis sublime
  When thus they meet in concord and good time.

The organ's pealing tones in grandeur rise,
  As to their seats the choir in order go,
They float and swell like incense to the skies,
  And over all subduing music throw,
  Now grandly loud and clear, now plaintive, soft and low.

Then solemnly the Vicar's voice is heard
  In accent's clear throughout the building's space,
Informing all that God's most holy Word
  " Doth bid us at all times to seek His face,"
  His people then invites unto " the throne of grace."

To which they all respond by kneeling there,
  And after him the solemn words repeat,
Imploring Him Whose presence everywhere
  And at all times the yearning heart doth greet,
  Despising none who come to worship at His feet.

The Curate then some wise selection reads,
    Some useful lesson from the holy book ;
Then earnestly again the Vicar pleads,
    As up to Heaven he casts imploring look,
    With Him Who never yet the earnest prayer mistook,

For that false sound which from the empty heart
    Sometimes, alas ! doth pain the listening ear
All meaningless ; devoid in every part
    Of worship's tone ; and bringing down, we fear,
    Condemnation only on those who there appear.

Then altogether in their places rise,
    And in sweet concord altogether sing,
Their rapt'rous voices surging to the skies,
    The organ's swelling notes resound and ring
    In sweetest unison, which heavenly blessings bring.

The Vicar then admonishes his flock
    In simple words which all can understand,
No flaming thunder-bolts his hearers shock,
    No red-winged light'nings and no burning brand
    By him in vengeance hurled with hard unsparing hand.

But earnest, forcible and moving speech,
    With soft persuasion and with kind appeal,
And stirring pathos he their hearts would reach
    To them his own true sympathy reveal
    Till all his fervour own and all his goodness feel.

The duties that each to the other owes,
    Exhorteth and enjoins them to fulfil ;
To all the source of consolation shows,
    Tells them how heavenly "love can work no ill"
    And with a joy divine each lonely heart doth fill.

The sermon o'er, the benediction then,
    In reverend tones to all he doth proclaim,
Just one brief sentence with a short "Amen,"
    Coupling the Godhead's awful, triune name
    Of " Father, Son and Spirit," evermore the same.

Then from the building to our homes we go,
  Remarking much on what we there have heard,
How lucidly the preacher's theme did show
  The hidden meaning of the mystic " Word,"
  Which worldly minds pronounce "unmeaning and absurd."

In future, distant and far-reaching times,
  When other people shall their spaces fill,
And other ears shall listen to the chimes
  Of their sweet bells ; our bodies cold and still
  Within the silent grave, devoid of life and will ;

When other voices shall in concert sing,
  And other hands the thrilling organ play,
And other preachers' telling accents ring
  Throughout the building in some future day,
  And other strangers there with purpose chance to stray;

The one good name upon the tablets there,
  Which he may scan with keen enquiring eye,
And reverend spirit in each house of prayer,
  Whose spires point upwards to the distant sky
  Where the dear dead are gone for whom at times we sigh.

The one good name which there shall meet his gaze,
  Engraven plainly on the plate of brass,
And shall the mind's sure admiration raise,
  Not his alone, but others who may pass
  And the inscription read ; each, all and ev'ry class.

" R.B.'s" initials or the full surname,
  Shall most distinctly to that age declare,
From whose munificence these churches came,
  At whose sole bidding rose each house of prayer
  The other items show just when he lived and where.

He built the churches and he built the schools,
  Where little children life's first lessons learn,
By sure and certain never-failing rules,
  Which at their peril unwise teachers spurn
  And unto methods false the mind's attention turn.

We give him honour and his praise we sing ;
  (Perhaps his praises have been sung before)
In tuneful verse our tribute we will bring
    And weave a garland as we sing and soar,
    With which we will him crown as our laudations pour.

O Mortimer ! like her of old thou art,
  By privilege exalted to the skies,
O ! (unlike her) act well thy noble part ;
    Thy priv'leges improve and thou shalt rise
    Into still grander life, the race's goal and prize.

THE RUINS.

Hard by is that old Roman camp and site
  Called "Silchester"; whereon long ages since
A war-like people dwelt ; by power of might
    Their conquests gained ; their legions did evince
    Both hardihood and courage, warrior and prince.

And who would think, but for the proofs around,
  In massive walls with ivy overgrown,
And interesting relics that are found
    Beneath the surface ; silver, bronze and stone
    Wrought into useful shapes and in museum shown ;

Hard wood, bright ivory and polished steel,
  Bone implements and even precious gold
Their hidden depths disclose and yet reveal,
    As they fresh treasures give and still unfold
    Their antiquarian wealth, by pick and spade unrolled ;

D

Who would believe amid the silence there,
  The peaceful quietude that reigns around,
Where nothing but its hoary walls declare,
  And what beneath its surface has been found
  That *there* a city flourished on that spot of ground ?

That *there* were streets, shops, houses, market stores,
  Fair thriving commerce and all-busy trade,
That labour sweating at its many pores,
  Its brawny arms and muscles there displayed
  And independent sloth on softest couches laid ?

That *there* young children in the streets did play,
  With merry gambol and loud ringing mirth,
And tott'ring age did wend its feeble way
  With falt'ring steps, low bending to the earth ;
  That *there* the poor once dwelt and those of noble birth ?

What wondrous changes time's resistless sweep
  Through lapse of ages does effect and bring ;
What transformations, sometimes burying deep
  In dark oblivion, as a trifling thing,
  Cities and their peoples, 'neath its all-brooding wing.

Here dwelt a people, classic and renowned,
  (Old Rome was classic as was Greece before)
More cultured people could not then be found,
  Well versed in arts, as also learning's lore ;
  A valiant people, too, their arms they proudly bore.

The early Britons they did dispossess,
  And for a while were masters of the place ;
The British at that time were little less
  Than savages ; "an undeveloped race
  With noble qualities." So history puts their case.

Our rude ancestors, although strong and brave,
  Were yet untrained in war's superior arts,
And though most gallantly they did behave,
  Sustaining well with most courageous hearts   [darts ;
  The onslaught of their foes, with shields and spears and

Yet were they all unequal in the strife,
  No match for Rome's all-conquering forces there ;
'Mid fearful carnage yielding up their life,
  Their homes defending with a courage rare,
  As taunted by their foes and madden'd by despair.

Thus did the Romans Britain then subdue,
  And subjugate it to their will and sway ;
They noble cities built and peopled, too,
  All through the land push'd their victorious way ;
  'Twas then " Calleva " rose, whose fate I sing to-day.

What mighty builders those old Romans were,
  How solid and substantial all they wrought ;
Take but a glimpse of Silchester, and there
  You will perceive that which surpasses thought,
  That which defies old Time and ne'er can come to nought.

What massive walls that city did enclose,
  Protecting it from panic or surprise,
Whene'er besieged by stern relentless foes
  Like maddened wolves with hungry glaring eyes,
  Whose tongues would lick their jaws in prospect of the prize.

Huge flints and flags alternately were laid,
  Imbedded in cement, which like a rock remains ;
Both broad and high, invulnerable were made ;
  All good material which still retains
  Its flint-like properties and wear and tear sustains.

Still grandly there that hoary wall appears,
  Tall trees like towers upon its ramparts grow,
After a lapse of fifteen hundred years
  All indestructible ; and still doth show
  A massive frowning front, that once defied the foe.

And what stupendous gates did shut them in,
  When night's dark shadows o'er the earth were thrown,
When fears were rife as darkness did begin
  To sway its sceptre from its ebon throne,
  Enshrouding with its gloom this semi-northern zone.

What powerful hinges must those gates have borne,
   Supporting well their huge and pond'rous weight,
On which with freedom they each smiling morn
    Wide open swung ; as when the day was late
    Closed and securely barred was then each city gate.

The spaces yet remain where they were hung,
   North, east, south, west, a spacious gap appears,
Wherein in centuries long past they swung ;
    A mighty vista, misty with the years
    Accumulated there ; all silent to the ears.

Its leading streets did at right angles run,
   Across the city from each distant gate,
Each other intersecting ; and each one
    Was neatly laid ; all even, true and straight,
    And all looked picturesque in that old Roman state.

Their architecture, too, was most sublime,
   Superb and elegant ; contrasting well
With many buildings of a later time,
    Whose ugly forms do yet remain to tell
    Their careless workmanship ; which these do much excel.

There was the " Forum," with its courts of law,
   And fine " Basilica " all cluster'd round,
Whose great attractions did attention draw ;
    Within their precincts there were often found
    The learned and the great ; the freeman and the bound.

Here likely Titus and Vespasian met
   After the carnage in the " Holy Land,"
Where Jews and Romans were in battle set,
    When these respectively did take command
    And their own forces led against the Jews, last stand.

Here, too, most probably the cruel laws,
   That were enacted in the " bloody " reign
Of Diocletian, 'gainst the sacred cause
    Of Him who suffer'd hunger, scorn and pain,
    And on Golgotha's hill was crucified and slain ;

Yes, here those laws were rigidly enforced
   Against the " Galilean's " foll'wers there ;
Pains were inflicted, wrongs were then endorsed,
   Insults with patience they did meekly bear,
   And on their foreheads thus His mystic name did wear.

Yonder the " Temple," a most classic fane,
   In shape polygonal, nor round nor square
But many-sided ; and did thus maintain
   A close resemblance by the builder's care
   To truth itself ; whose angles meet us ev'rywhere.

Here the " Amphitheatre " imposing stood,
   A huge round building most conspicuous there,
Tow'ring above its fellows as it should ;
   Broad at the base with spacious dome and rare :
   Did much impress the sight and noble aspect wear.

Within this vast enclosure seats were ranged,
   Tier upon tier up to the bending roof,
Where pleasantly bright thoughts were interchanged,
   With spice of wit and mutual behoof
   By those who from the poor then proudly held aloof.

Down in the bottom a large open space,
   Stretched from the centre to the sloping seats,
Where with much nimbleness and agile grace
   Were then perform'd some most astounding feats,
   As man with savage brute in deadly combat meets.

There slaves sometimes with hornëd cattle fought,
   Attracting them with bright red flaming cloth,
Which, when the brute would charge the man, was caught
   Upon its horns ; as with mad fury wroth
   Its nostrils did distend, its mouth all foam and froth.

There Gladiators fought with beasts of prey,
   Whose dreadful forms did at the gates appear,
Where they their teeth and talons did display,
   And roar aloud which smote the list'ning ear
   With terror's wild affright sounding so close and near.

There well equipped, with spear and spreading shield
  The warrior stood ; while twice ten thousand eyes
Upon him turn'd ; anxious to see him wield
  With much dexterity 'mid howls and cries
  The long and tap'ring lance, which flashes as it flies.

The ravenous beast all madden'd for the fray,
  By being kept from food for hours before,
Springs, leaps and bounds soon as the bolt gives way
  Which erst had held the cage's massive door
  Into the open space with loud and angry roar.

With tail erect and flying mane outspread,
  With flaming eyes and jaws extended wide,
The lion madly by his hunger led
  Flies to the combat ; in his strength and pride
  Disdaining him who thus his fury had defied.

All breathless with excitement yonder throng,
  Crane out their necks and strain their anxious eyes
To witness that which they had waited long ;
  The victor's triumph, when the vanquish'd dies,
  The lion or the man in death's embraces lies.

The monster comes, the hero steps aside,
  And lightly prods him with his pointed spear ;
The lion slips, which wounds his kingly pride,
  Springs to his feet and rushing madly near
  Receives a piercing thrust, incisive, sharp and clear.

Stung by the pain, he howls and groans and cries.
  His streaming blood now mingles with the dust ;
Yet unsubdued his long tail whisks and flies,
  Again he comes, and one deep fearful thrust
  Lets out the precious life ; he dies because he must.

From that vast multitude there then ascend,
  Loud ringing cheers and shouts of wild applause ;
Ten thousand voices all together blend
  In celebration of the victor's cause
  Who by his valiant deeds had thus escaped death's jaws.

Not always thus, though, would the contest end,
  And sometimes sick'ning sights were witness'd there ;
Horror to pain its ghastly aid would lend,
  Chilling the ardour of the young and fair
  Who shrank in deep dismay from this fell deadly pair.

In that arena sometimes there was seen
  Sights that the flowing blood would freeze and chill,
When by some accident the man has been
  Thrown from his feet ; sensation then would fill
  All sympathetic hearts ; the mad beast charge at will.

With teeth and fangs the brute the man would tear,
  Who at his mercy scrambles on the floor,
His prostrate foe he will in no wise spare,
  Tortures and grips him with a growling roar
  Until his strength all spent he welters in his gore.

The carcass then with savage fury he
  Would toss and turn and tear it limb from trunk,
Devour his flesh with much carniv'rous glee,
  Lick up his blood till with it he was drunk
  Enjoying much the feast ; from which in horror shrunk

The sensitive and tender-hearted there ;
  Appalled and sicken'd at the ghastly scene,
Pale with excitement at the dreadful scare
  Turn from the sight with most disgusted mien :
  Such brutalizing sports at Silchester have been.

And oft 'twould happen that the slave who bore,
  The blood-red cloth to irritate the bull,
To stir his rage and to inflame him more,
  Till he with fury should be mad and full
  And charge with desperation his tormentor's skull ;

'Twould sometimes happen that the cloth would fly
  All on one side and swerve and flutter round,
And he who threw it the next moment lie
  Trampled and torn and bleeding on the ground :
  All disembowelled there with moaning, dying sound.

Thus revell'd Rome in those far-distant days
    At Silchester; in all the pomp and pride
Of earthly glory; all the glare and blaze
    Of ancient splendour; through its streets did ride
    Emperors and monarchs with courtiers at their side.

Who would believe it? I again would ask,
    But for the proofs and evidences there,
That to the excavator's pleasing task
    So freely yield their hidden beauties rare
    In bones, and rings, and coins, and Roman earthenware.

How eloquent was that discovered tile,
    On which some am'rous swain the word did write
" *Puellam*," or " My Lass," in simple style,
    Thinking of her who absent from his sight
    Did yet his being fill with love's most sweet delight.

Ah! little did he think when that sweet word
    He lightly scratched upon that earthen plate,
That 'twould again long ages hence be heard,
    And be repeated at some distant date
    Of near two thousand years succeeding to their fate.

Trade implements, shop fittings, bolts and keys,
    Steel-yards, flesh-hooks and many oyster shells,
Proving that "natives" even then could please
    And charm the appetite; their presence tells
    Epicurean tales, of Roman beaux and belles.

Hones, mortars, bracelets, and some finger-rings,
    All kinds of tools and even plast'rers' floats,
"Still bearing marks of colour"; all this brings
    Most clearly to the mind of him who notes
    Proof irresistible of that which this denotes.

Some iron styli and fine Samian ware,
    A large lead pipe and tubing made of glass;
Some funeral urns have also been found there;
    A "bar of silver," and some plates of brass;
    All which with care we note as on we slowly pass.

Cooking utensils, broken pots and pans,
  Some drinking vessels, cups and pitchers too ;
Domestic articles, including fans,
    With which the ladies would the breezes woo
    When Sol's exhausting rays did stream from yonder blue.

Some roofing tiles and handsome Roman bricks,
  And tiles for paving of superb design ;
Coins of all kinds here strangely intermix
    From old Augustas, down to Constantine,
    Vespasian and Trajan ; Blandius and Valentine.

Maximiamus and Honorius,
  Of Commodus and Theodosius too,
Marc Antony and Carausius,
    Of Julius Cæsar ; and away all through
    The Roman occupation : giving each his due.

Here, too, a prize that may be termed "unique,"
  Within the " Forum " was discovered there ;
All over Europe we in vain might seek
    For such a treasure, so exceeding rare :   [care
    'Twas hail'd with much delight. 'Tis kept with pride and

In yonder mansion, at old Stratfieldsaye.
  In some well-chosen and appointed place,
Its beauties as of old to still display ;
    Of form and figure and artistic grace
    As when it first was modelled by that war-like race.

The Legionary Eagle, Rome's Ensign ;
  Which oft in battle they had proudly borne,
As then each column in unbroken line
    Did march in order to the sounding horn
    Or bugle's shriller blast whose echoes woke the morn.

Of purest bronze, its light wings tipt with gold,
  But which, alas ! some vandal had destroyed
Or thrown away, or for a trifle sold,
    By means of which some pleasure was enjoyed
    By this iconoclast, thus ruthlessly employed.

The Legion's "honours" on its gilded wings
   Were finely traced; then proudly overhead
Upon a "thunderbolt," while music rings
   'Twould flash and gleam, as by the standard led,
   Those warriors of old fought till the field was red

With blood and reeking carnage of their foes;
   The gallant Britons, who did then defend
With noble daring as their courage rose
   Their primitive rude huts; with valour blend
   Unconquerable will on to the bitter end.

These things all indicate that here there dwelt
   A teeming population; and we know
That it was Roman; not the early Celt
   Whose *previous earthworks yet remain* to show
   How nobly once they fought long centuries ago.

Yes, here dwelt Rome for full four hundred years,
   And most indelibly their name they wrote;
On all around their impress still appears
   In walls and relics; all which do denote
   How once they lived and toiled and did on pleasure dote.

But what a change! A deadly silence now
   Reigns o'er the "city" that once swarm'd with life;
Gloomy and sullen is its sombre brow,
   Stillness and quietude o'er all are rife
   Where once a people dwelt renowned for war's stern strife.

The sweep of centuries has brushed aside,
   This ancient people who did dispossess
The Celtic owners, and their rights denied
   And of all ownership did them divest,
   Demolishing their huts by edict's stern behest.

They have themselves in turn been driven out,
   And scatter'd by the winds of time and change;
Where once was heard their all-victorious shout,
   The peaceful Briton can now freely range,
   Attend his flocks and herds and cultivate his grange.

Time's retributive and all-powerful hand,
  Metes out destruction as the ages roll,
On those who once did desolate the land
  For love of conquest and unjust control,
  As roughshod o'er mankind they sought the distant goal.

Those mighty cities of the hoary past,
  Rome, Nineveh, and Babylon and Tyre,
Have all departed and their glory cast
  Into oblivion's shade ; their names expire
  'Neath Time's all-blasting breath and stern avenging ire.

Let England, too, take heed and ponder well,
  The lessons taught by these dynastic fates ;
For although now securely she doth dwell
  Peace and prosperity within her gates,
  What seer shall dare make known what yet for her awaits?

Her present actions shall her future fate
  Determine and decide ; she must beware
How she doth treat those she doth subjugate
  In other lands ; in Africa take care
  How she doth intermeddle with the races there.

They must be ruled with *gentle* if firm hand,
  Their rights must be respected by our laws ;
It should be borne in mind that 'tis *their* land,
  We but intruders ; though we claim our cause
  To be a just one ; free from imperfection's flaws.

Equitable returns we must them make
  For what from them in trade we may receive ;
By force or fraud *by no means* may we take
  That which is theirs ; nor must we them deceive
  If we would have them trust us and our word believe.

Let no dishonour our escutcheon stain,
  Let no harsh treatment our good name impair ;
Unjust, aggressive, wanton acts restrain
  Which only leave a bad impression there
  Upon the native mind committed to our care.

If Africa is "dark," then England must be light ;
  ('Tis by comparison we find it so)
Her reputation is for truth and right ;
  To those in darkness she her light must show
  And round each weaker race her strong protection throw.

If otherwise she acts and does ignore
  Humanity's just claims in other lands,
Where most beseechingly they us implore,
  And "Ethiopia stretches out her hands,"
  Where with the lash and scourge Oppression's tyrant stands:

If with high hand and proud imperious sway,
  She tramples on their rights and treads them down
And to their cries does no attention pay,
  But 'mid war's clangour their strong pleadings drown,
  Destroy their huts and homes and all their kings uncrown ;

And take by force that which to them belongs
  Without regard to equity and right,
Inflict upon them cruelties and wrongs,
  For love of conquest and display of might ;
  It will be noted well by the all-seeing sight

Of Him Whose presence everywhere pervades,
  In heaven above and on the earth below,
In clearest light and 'mid the deepest shades ;
  He Whom our inmost thoughts can read and know,
  From Whom we cannot hide nor from His presence go:

And "with what measure we to them may mete,
  It shall be measured out to us again,"
Until our own discomfiture complete
  And we just recompense of Him obtain
  Our Empire's strength decline and all its glory wane.

And like those nations of the mighty past,
  Whose once great names did hold the world in awe,
Who thought their grandeur would for ever last
  And all their edicts were eternal law ;
  Round England too like these Fate her dark curtain draw.

Armies and navies may be very well
    And both be useful in their proper sphere,
Thrilling accounts respectively may tell,
    Of stern engagements with their foemen near
    And splendid actions won ; all which with pride we hear :

But 'tis not these that make a nation strong,
    Howe'er efficient and well-mann'd they be,
'Tis not to these protection doth belong ;
    Not these alone from danger can set free
    When foes around us swarm this island of the sea.

'Tis *character* the most that can insure
    A people's safety and true progress here ;
'Tis *righteousness* alone that can procure
    Exemption from disquietude and fear ;
    Virtue alone is strong : Our duty then is clear

Both to ourselves and those beneath our sway,
    To cultivate a love for truth and right,
And at all times the " golden law " obey ;
    To those in darkness show the friendly light :
    In *these alone* consist a nation's strength and might.

If England, led by its illustrious Queen,
    These principles shall practice and revere,
If to strong virtue's side she ever lean
    To honesty and purity adhere,
She like a rock shall stand.   Sin only need she fear.

OCTOBER.

October now once more appears,
The autumn has come round again ;
The laws that rule the circling spheres,
Uphold the earth and bind the main,
The months in quick succession bring :
It seems but yesterday 'twas spring.

But spring and summer both are gone,
The autumn too is on the wing ;
The falling leaves bestrew the lawn,
The nightingales no longer sing :
The Robin (lovely autumn bird),
Is now the songster chiefly heard.

While southwardly the sun declines,
And objects lengthened shadows throw ;
The coming winter gives some signs,
That we its near approach may know ;
The trees are growing nude and bare
And colder is the midnight air.

Upon the housetops day by day,
Behold the swallows now appear,
And twitter each a simple lay,
That seems to tell the falling year ;
By wondrous instinct 'tis they know
The time has come when they must go.

The mud nest built beneath the eaves,
Or in the humble barn or shed,
Reluctantly each bird now leaves,
Where each was reared, and nursed and fed,
And all in council seem to sit,
Deliberating as they twit.

O ! 'tis an animating sight
To watch them as they thus appear ;
When spreads the morning's golden light,
And fogs and mists begin to clear,
They stretch their wings as ships their sails,
And wait like them the fav'ring gales.

Unnumbered pinions beat the air,
And flap and flutter to the sight,
As crowding altogether there
(Their wings I note are black and white),
They seem to talk their prospects o'er,
And twitter, twitter, more and more.

Then all at once away they fly
To Southern regions bright and fair :
They quit awhile this wintry sky,
And bask in genial radiance there ;
Over the distant waters go,
And thus escape the frost and snow.

'Tis pleasant at this season too
To take a walk at early morn,
When all the hedges lined with dew ;
The spider's webs among the thorn,
So neatly and so deftly wrought,
As though by skill of studied thought.

Ten thousand precious crystals shine,
Reflecting each the light of day ;
Each sep'rate web, each single line
Is laden with the filmy spray,
Which glitters in the morning sun,
And helps to show how webs are spun.

And who that sees, but must admire,
The wondrous instinct spiders show ;
They labour on and never tire,
Their threads they fasten as they go ;
They hitch them here, and hitch them there,
And loop them all round everywhere.

Round and round the spider goes,
In circles he his web doth spin;
His wondrous skill in weaving shows,
His threads are strong though they are thin;
Now right across the web he takes,
The slender cord which never breaks.

This artist needs no tools nor light,
With both of these he can dispense;
He works his wonders in the night,
When steeped is every human sense
In all composing soothing sleep:
Save those who wakeful vigils keep.

One calls thee "magic artizan,"
And well thou dost deserve the name;
The more thy wondrous work we scan,
The more ourselves are put to shame;
Thy instinct baffles human thought,
So strangely neat thy web is wrought.

The main threads at right angles run,
And stretch across from side to side;
On these the other lines are spun,
Securely fastened, neatly tied;
Till the whole network is complete,
The central cord and dark retreat:

Where hides the spider all day long,
As hides a wild beast in his lair;
Till in the web's own meshes strong,
Some thoughtless insect struggles there;
The motion vibrates to the den,
And down the spider rushes then.

He knows his web hath caught the prey,
Convulsive twitchings tell him so;
And down he comes intent to slay,
A merciless unsparing foe;
As shoots a meteor in the sky,
So darts the spider on the fly.

He grips it fast with all his might,
Nor heeds its agonizing cries,
Then round its body firm and tight,
A powerful cord securely ties ;
He binds its legs, he binds its wings,
And wraps it round with finest strings.

From his own body neatly spun,
The thread requir'd to bind the prey,
Forthwith is wrought ; the work is done ;
The victim then is dragged away ;
Connecting it with his own rear,
Both fly and spider disappear.

Though tragic is the poor fly's end,
We much admire the spider's skill ;
He is indeed to man a friend,
Though oft we treat him very ill ;
The flies we say (or think at least),
A nuisance are to man and beast.

Then how delightful as we go,
And take our walk the woods among ;
Where nature holds a fairy show,
The trees with varied colours hung ;
The leaves are red, white, pink and grey,
Thus beauty waits upon decay.

Such gorgeous colours now are seen,
As by the artist never yet
Or limner, howe'er skill'd, have been
Upon the outstretched canvas set ;
Art may not rival Nature's power,
As seen in ev'ry leaf and flower.

A gentle breeze now stirs the air,
The leaves fall softly to the ground,
And being dry they rustle there,
And make a most delightful sound ;
They float and flutter left and right,
They charm the ear and please the sight.

E

O ! peaceful is the wood's retreat,
And sacred is the silence there ;
Now broken only by the sweet
Reverberations in the air ;
From birds that chatter wild and free
And sport themselves on ev'ry tree.

The jay screams out with mad delight,
The magpie answers to his mate ;
The merry squirrel comes in sight,
And throws a nutshell on your pate ;
Then laughing wildly off he goes,
And drops another on your nose.

And now the cooings of the dove,
Break pleasantly upon the ear ;
The turtle whispers to his love,
And she is glad that he is near :
In mutual peace and calm content,
These happy creatures' lives are spent.

Now o'er my path a rabbit runs,
And instantly is out of sight ;
My presence 'tis the creature shuns,
It has no other cause for flight :
Though did it know me it might stay,
Nor make such haste to get away.

And now a tapping noise I hear,
And looking round to find the cause,
I notice on the old trunk near
A creature hanging by its claws ;
The woodpecker, 'tis he, 'tis he,
That hammers thus upon the tree.

He searches 'mid the broken bark,
For insects that are hiding there ;
Then thrusts his beak into the dark
And drags them from their hidden lair :
He takes the vermin by surprise,
His beak is strong and clear his eyes.

Out in the open now I go,
And leave the wood with all its charms ;
The autumn sun is all aglow,
I stand and gaze with folded arms
Upon the beauties that I see,
Hill, dale and copse and grassy lea.

The streamlet murmurs in its bed,
The sheep are bleating in the fold ;
The rooks are cawing overhead,
And quite a concert seem to hold ;
They caw and caw as round they fly
And soar yet higher in the sky.

The cattle graze in yonder mead
And roam beneath a cloudless sky,
On tender herbs and grass they feed ;
Or chew the cud as down they lie.
And free from anxious carking care,
They rest in calm contentment there.

The patient horses, side by side,
Do nibble each the other's neck ;
And seem to take a loving pride
In pulling at each other's fleck ;
Upon the withers 'tis they feel
An irritation this can heal.

And now perhaps in groups they stand,
Each head turned to the other's tail,
The quiet creatures understand
How best the flies they can assail ;
And with their brushes gently fan,
Each other's face as best they can.

With streaming mane and forelock now,
They canter wildly, freely there ;
Till up the hill and on the brow,
Then stop, and sniff, and snort, and stare ;
As though they fancied they could see
A foe in ev'ry spreading tree.

And then as though by fear impelled,
With one consent away they bound ;
By no vain trappings they are held,
They fling their heels and tear the ground :
A noble creature is the horse,
Endued with wondrous speed and force.

The busy hum of yonder town,
Falls faintly on the list'ning ear ;
Where men of learning and renown,
Their monuments to science rear ;
Where thriving commerce leads the way,
And capital doth labour pay.

Where competition fierce and keen
And trade with trade contending strives,
And flowing down the streets are seen
The streams of precious human lives ;
From tributary side-streets they,
Converge upon the broadest way.

There, lounging at the corners stand,
The parasites of human life ;
The curse of ev'ry clime and land,
The scourge of ev'ry honest wife ;
The men who neither work nor pray,
But fritter all their lives away.

With hands into their pockets thrust,
And foul pipe stuck within their jaws,
The slaves of all corrupting lust ;
They serve no honest useful cause :
Rank weeds are they in life's great field,
Or trees that only poisons yield.

They are the refuse and the scum,
Civilization's direful bane ;
In town's and cities 'tis they come,
With all their pestilential train :
A tribute to the pauper's cause,
A menace to their country's laws.

But this no rural picture is,
I therefore am digressing now,
And back 'mid scenes of rustic bliss,
Where graze the horse, the ox and cow ;
My fancy shall my footsteps lead,
'Tis there my muse delights to feed.

And yonder in the distance there,
A flock of gabbling geese I see ;
Their merry cacklings fill the air,
They all are happy as can be :
They spread their wings and strut about,
They waddle in and waddle out.

Now to the pond they wend their way,
Then all at once they take to flight,
And helter skelter, wildly they,
Flap their broad pinions to the sight ;
They stretch their necks and loudly scream,
Till down they settle in the stream.

The farms are stacked with golden corn,
All thatched and trimm'd and looking neat ;
The hedger clips the sprouting thorn,
The engine thrashes out the wheat ;
The elevator takes the straw,
The sacks hold all the corn we saw.

O ! how I love to hear the hum,
While walking leisurely along ;
As o'er the field the murmurs come,
And tune my heart to grateful song :
The engine snorts, coughs, pants and blows,
And on the merry labour goes.

The men stand high upon the stack,
And pitch the bunches down below ;
The brown grain falls into the sack,
Stretched open to receive it so :
And up the elevator quick,
The straw is carried to the rick.

In yonder field I notice now
The labourer marking out the "lands;"
With horse accustomed to the plough
And guided well with steady hands,
He makes a rude gash in the field,
That did such golden harvest yield.

He flips his reins, "come hither" cries,
As o'er the yellow ground he goes;
While overhead with hungry eyes,
Are troops of all-devouring crows;
That swarm upon his flank and rear,
And worms and grubs soon disappear.

He parcels out the land in strips,
And round each strip untiring goes;
With merry heart he lightly trips,
And sings or whistles what he knows:
Till one whole "land" completely done,
At once another is begun.

A few yards off again he starts,
The clods slope upwards from below,
And each "land" from the other parts,
A wise arrangement this we know;
A channel broad, and deep is seen,
To cleave the "lands" and run between.

When winter comes with heavy rains,
Succeeded by the frost and snow;
And deluged are the roads and plains,
As down the streaming torrents flow:
The seeds might never come to birth,
But rot and perish in the earth.

The ploughman wisely this foresees
And tills his land as I have shown,
And down the channels run with ease
All unimpeded and alone,
The surplus waters from the soil:
Which otherwise the crops might spoil.

And O ! how picturesque it looks,
Thus parcelled out and neatly done ;
And how delighted are the rooks,
As down they settle one by one,
They dig their beaks into the ground,
And thus the worms and grubs are found.

Straight as an arrow ev'ry line,
Unerring is the ploughman's eye ;
And brightly does the ploughshare shine,
As lightning flashes in the sky :
And shine the rooks and shine the clods,
And shine the worms beneath the sods.

O ! how delightful thus to roam,
Upon a lovely autumn day ;
With all one's faculties at home,
To make each object tribute pay,
That one may meet with in one's course,
And feel no pang of vain remorse.

Now sinks the sun in yonder west,
And paints in beauty all the skies ;
And there in silv'ry splendours drest,
Behold the full-orbed moon arise ;
The stars are hidden by her light,
And in the distance skulks the night.

And now the bats flit to and fro,
They cannot bear the light of day ;
But wait until the sun is low,
Then wander forth in search of prey :
They chase the chafers in the air,
And dart with wondrous swiftness there.

But I must to my home return,
And lay my body down to rest ;
For home the human heart doth yearn,
Of all earth's places 'tis the best :
However poor the home may be,
'Tis home we all desire to see.

My ramble in the woods and fields,
Along the road and by the stream ;
Matter for meditation yields,
And call forth gratitude to Him
Who made the world so wondrous fair,
And made all creatures happy there.

NOTE.—A copy of the above was forwarded to H.R.H.
Princess Beatrice in connection with her visit to Reading,
and the following reply received :—

HENRY 3RD TOWER,
WINDSOR CASTLE,
Dec. 9th, 1889.

Lady Biddulph is desired by Her Royal Highness
Princess Beatrice to thank Mr. J. Mosdell for the verses he
has kindly sent to Her Royal Highness, and for all his
kind wishes.

HUNTLEY AND PALMERS' GREAT BISCUIT MANUFACTORY.

O ! who has not heard of old Reading's famed town,
  So widely made known by the industry there,
Whose goods are sent forth both east, west, south and north,
  And with which for quality none can compare.

'Tis built on the banks of old Kennet's fair stream,
  And 'tween it the river doth silently flow ;
Neat bridges stretch o'er, thus connecting each shore,
  Their useful long arms o'er the waters they throw.

And on either side spacious buildings appear,
   Which cover vast acres of wide stretching space ;
With red brick and stone, due proportion is shown,
   And all well arranged in their own proper place.

Tall shafts tow'ring upwards and piercing the sky,
   Like mainmasts that stretch from the deck down below;
Whence borne far away where with clouds it can play,
   The smoke in huge columns doth heavenwards go.

And O ! what machinery working within,
   In seeming confusion that puzzles the mind ;
How it rattles and hums, its rollers and drums
   And slow trav'lling ovens that evermore wind.

Long straps straight or twisted on wheels large and small,
   All which go one way when the straps travel straight,
But when they are changed and inversely arranged
   The wheels are reversed with bewildering rate.

The thud of the " cutters," the roll of the cogs,
   The creak and the whizz of the straps as they fly ;
While long sheets of dough up the canvas now go
   All spotless and pure from the " rollers " close by.

No firm equal to it old England can boast,
   Nor indeed can the world its rival e'er show ;
Where biscuits and cakes of all sizes and makes
   Impregnate the air with the odours they throw.

Of cakes there are " Bristol," " Madeira " and " Lunch,"
   The " Reading," the " Currant," the " Plain " and the
     " Seed ;"
" Fruit," " Almond " and " Rice," " Banquet," " Diet " and
     " Ice,"
   All which are of excellent flavour indeed.

" Sultana," " Sponge," " Wedding," " Queen's Heart,"
     " Battenburg,"
     " Genoa," " Lucerne," " Eton," " Orange " and " Snow ;"
" Milan," " Cocoanut," (for the palace or hut),
     " Sandringham," " Lisbon," " Cambridge," " Rugby " also.

" Chatsworth " and " Valencia " and " Lemon " as well,
  "Teacakes," "Tops and Bottoms" and others unknown,
Whose virtues are such connoisseurs praise them much
  At home and abroad in each wide spreading zone.

The names of the biscuits, suffice it to say,
  (They also are nourishing, wholesome and good)
Shall here "legion" be ; o'er each far distant sea
  Their merits are known as an excellent food.

O ! gigantic firm ! 'tis the stay of the town,
  Without it we could not long very well do ;
If once it should fail it would sure to entail
  Disaster wide-spread and much suffering too.

So huge in proportions, so many employed,
  All nations draw thence their much-needed supplies ;
World-wide is the fame of the Palmers' good name
  Who manage so ably this vast enterprize.

"The hand of the diligent 'tis maketh rich,"
  In them we have evidence of this great truth ;
Most industrious they both by night and by day,
  In life's early manhood and even in youth.

And they as a consequence often have " stood
  Before kings" and princes with much lawful pride :
Who sometimes have come from their far distant home
  Across the blue waters from earth's farther side,

To see the great works of these now famous men,
  Their huge manufactory outside and in,
Whose labour employs women, girls, men and boys,
  Where hundreds and thousands their daily bread win.

Where biscuits are made to supply the whole world,
  From " Dan to Beersheba," "O Groat's to Land's End ;"
Borne out on the breeze to "the isles of the seas"
  All round the great globe their confections they send.

On yonder plantation the hard toiling slave,
  Allowed a few moments can crack up his " Lunch ;"
The hunter afar with wild nature at war
  "Tea," " Coffee," or " Osborne" can quietly munch.

The boy in the cabin, the " watch " on the deck,
   The passengers lounging in comfort below,
In spacious saloon, all regard them a boon,
   For biscuits and wine much respect seem to show.

In tropical regions and cold frigid zones,
   In temperate climates and both hemispheres;
On Africa's plains and where stern winter reigns
   In Lapland and Greenland their presence appears.

On yon western prairies, in far Eastern climes,
   New Guinea, Borneo and Madagascar ;
To distant Cape Horn and Cape Colony borne
   And where " spicy breezes " are scented afar.

Remote Australasia, New Zealand close by,
   And there where the Southern Cross glistens and glows ;
In Russia's cold land and on Afric's hot sand
   And where the Atlantic its wild fury shows.

Fair Constantinople, Siberia's wastes,
   The Chinese Empire and old Persia's estate ;
Chili and Peru and the Argentine too
   On all these the " Export " departments await.

All tribes of the earth and all peoples and tongues,
   The red-skinned American and the Hindu ;
The dark sons of Ham and of distant Siam,
   The Hottentot, Caffirs and Macalulu.

The Pigmies, the Dwarfs, and thick-set Esquimaux,
   The tall Patagonians over the seas ;
Maories, Zulus, and the down-trodden Jews,
   These goods never fail to entice and to please.

The swarthy Arabian, dusky Malay,
   The tawny Mongolian there in the East;
The hordes of Tartar in the desert afar
   These goods are to them a perpetual feast.

The noble Circassian, " Celestial " Chinee,
   The sensuous Turk and the small Japanese ;
The Calmucks as well shall the list help to swell,
   All fair Europeans including with these.

Thus, then, this large firm all earth's races supply
  With "Albert," with "Brighton," with "Bath" and
    "Cheapside ;"
"Fancy Rout," "Macaroon" and the sweet "Demi Lune"
  And dear "Littlefolk" and the "Household" beside.

"Jamaica," "Pearl," "Button Nuts," "Honey Drops,"
  "Maziena," "Empire," "Combination" and "Queen ;"
"Milk," "Camp," "Ratafias," "Captain," "Cuddy" and
    "Cheese,"
  "Rich Travellers," "Riveria," "Picnic," "Madeline."

"Nonpareil," "German Rusks" and "Caricature,"
  "Digestive," "Colonial," "Nonsuch" and "Savoy ;"
"Filbert," "Diadem," and the neat little "Gem,"
  "Snowflake," "Smyrna," "Social," "Swiss," "Toast,"
    "Cracknell Toy."

"Caprice," "Abernethy," "Tea Rusks," "Almond Rings,"
  "Brown College," "Meat Wafers" and "Ice Wafers" too ;
"Walnut," "Arrowroot," "Universal" and "Fruit,"
  "Thin Captain," "Presburg," all most sweet, fresh and new.

"Salt," "Sicily Nuts," "Water," "Wheaten," "Wheatmeal,"
  "Nic Nac," "Kinder Garten," the "Oaten" and "Roll ;"
"Moss," "Tourist," "Bodour," and a vast number more,
  I here have but mentioned a half of the whole.

All honour to those who by toil have thus raised
  So useful a monument to their own worth ;
Preserving their name and recording their fame
  Which already reaches the ends of the earth.

Already their name is in lands far away
  Familiar as father and brother and friend ;
Far over the sea the well-known "H. and P.,"
  Are quite household words and a charm to life lend.

In summer and winter, at home and abroad,
  In each special season all through the short year,
When out on the lawn or when round the fire drawn
  These goods never fail to enspirit and cheer.

Excursions and picnics and holiday times
    The one indispensable article they ;
All over the earth at each marriage and birth,
    And even when death claims his own lawful prey.

When friend meets with friend or a neighbour looks in,
    When parents and brothers and sisters all meet
Their goodwill to show and much happiness know,
    Their presence is needed to make it complete.

And at stated times extra "orders" arrive,
    When Christmas approaches and wears out the year;
When Easter draws nigh and the sun rules the sky
    The days lengthen out and the mornings are clear.

'Tis then from all parts of the ponderous globe
    Most urgent requests are to hand by each mail ;
Both " Home " and " Export " for all kinds and each sort,
    And all are complied with at once without fail.

By letter and telegram ever they come,
    Away from "the uttermost parts of the earth " ;
The Antipodes far away o'er the seas,
    And where first the morning's glad beams have their birth.

And thence where the sun sinks the ocean behind,
    Across the Atlantic the missives arrive ;
Equator to Pole, the terraqueous whole,
    All, all, draw their stores from this great biscuit hive.

By " Orient " liner, " Cunard," cablegram,
    Upon the broad surface, or deep down below ;
By light'ning speed sent from each far continent
    And earth's many islands these messengers go.

Long live the good men who by dint of hard toil,
    Built up this colossal, gigantic concern ;
Whose labour employs women, girls, men and boys,
    And where many thousands their daily bread earn.

THE DESTRUCTION OF THE TAY BRIDGE AND THE LOSS OF A PASSENGER TRAIN.

December 28th, 1879.

———

The Tay Bridge has fallen ! how terribly shocking,
   What mortal but shudders to hear the sad tale ?
That splendid long Bridge in the wind 'gan a rocking,
   And fell with a crash by the force of the gale.

That dark stormy night we have cause to remember,
   When over our island a hurricane blew,
Which caused ere the closing of dreary December
   An accident frightful and ruinous too.

That glorious achievement of skill and of science,
   Which spann'd the broad river from " Bonnie Dundee,"
So graceful and strong as if bidding defiance
   To all the rude storms coming over the sea,

Destroy'd by the tempest, which raging in madness,
   Seized fast the high girders and rent them in twain ;
As Samson of old grasped the pillars in sadness
   And bowed with his might and died with the slain.

The Bridge shook and trembled, for now on its centre,
   The wind all its fury at once seemed to bear ;
And lo ! at this moment a train seen to enter'
   Gave force to the storm and destruction was there.

O ! horrid confusion ; crash ! down go the railings,
   The Train rushes into the dark foaming sea ;
No friends hear the shrieks or the heartrending wailings,
   And none are permitted the sad sight to see.

Down ! down to the dark seething boisterous waters,
   The carriages pitch with their sad human freight ;
Wives, husbands and children, sons, mothers and daughters,
   Who now are aware of their terrible fate.

But vain are their shrieks for none can now hear them,
    Their voices are hushed in the tempest's wild roar,
And mortals hear nought but the winds raving near them
    And voice of the sea as it breaks on the shore.

Oh ! what pen can describe the anticipations
    Of meeting with those whom they loved once again ;
The warm hearty welcomes, the fond salutations,
    To greet them as they shall alight from the train ?

There friend with his friend then to meet was expecting,
    And joyful bright thoughts flitted thro' the young brain ;
The mother was waiting, no danger suspecting,
    To press to her bosom her darling again.

Shut fast in the carriages filled with emotion,
    And thinking of pleasures that shortly would be,
When over this arm of the turbulent ocean
    Each friend and each lover each other should see.

The Driver stood well to the post of his duty,
    And fearlessly he the wild hurricane braved ;
He had in his keeping old age, youth and beauty,
    Who shudder'd as round them the mad tempest raved.

Though, doubtless, they thought not of danger impending,
    Believing the Bridge was intact and secure ;
Though nature's dread forces were with it contending,
    Serenely they thought 'twould those forces endure.

Far out on the Bridge human aid all denied them,
    Cut off from all help from each far distant shore,
Still hoping no evil that night would betide them,
    As round them the elements angrily roar.

And thinking of those who their coming awaited,
    The friends they should see when the journey was o'er,
By strong ties of friendship or kinship related,
    Whose presence so often had cheer'd them before.

There, all in good humour, unheeding the weather,
    Bright flashes of wit caused the ripple to flow,
And smart repartee as conversing together
    And on to their doom unsuspecting they go.

Grim Death in the darkness was crouching and hiding
   And wide he the gates of destruction had thrown,
And all in that ill-fated train who were riding
   That night he intended to claim as his own.

His claim he enforced as he all unexpected
   Stalked up in the gloom of that terrible night,
Obstructed their path and the train intercepted,   [flight.
   When hope plumed her pinions and spread them for

Oh ! terrible doom 'mid the storm's fearful raging,
   With frightful mad leap to destruction they go ;
No thought, sign or warning, disaster presaging,
   And no indication the danger to show.

Lock'd hopelessly in was life's all-precious treasure,
   And bounding along on their path o'er the main,
When (hushed be all revelry, music and pleasure)
   Down the dark gulf goes the ill-fated train.

A shower of sparks from the engine ascending
   Lit up for a moment the darkness and gloom ;
A flash and a glare told of mischief impending,
   Suggesting their fate and their tragical doom.

And those who were watching with much agitation
   And wondering what these strange things might portend,
Decided to seek more advantageous station
   And thither their footsteps accordingly bend.

The moon through dark clouds was now fitfully shining
   And running along by the foam-beaten shore,
They catch just a glimpse of the Bridge's outlining,
   Confirming suspicions indulged in before.

A fearful large gap just near where the Bridge centred
   Was dimly discerned through the gloom and the spray;
And death's dismal portals all suddenly entered
   And perished that night in the depths of the Tay.

And now over hill-top, through town and through city,
   Like wild-fire the tidings most rapidly spread ;
The Tay Bridge had fallen and still greater pity,
   That numbers had joined in the ranks of the dead.

And now on the shore anxious groups had assembled,
  Their faces all blanching with terror and fear,
At the wind and the spray they shivered and trembled ;
  But heeded them not nor the wild night so drear.

Their thoughts were all fixed on the Bridge that had broken,
  The train that had fallen headlong to the sea,
The friends that had perished, of whom not a token
  Nor vestige remaining could any one see.

They eagerly scan the broad face of the ocean,
  If haply some object afloat they may trace,
But nought can they learn 'mid the waves' seething motion
  Of this most alarming and pitiful case.

Thus wearily watching they linger till morning,
  Their hearts beating high with excitement and fear,
As thinking of those who that night without warning
  Sank down in the darkness and perished so near.

Oh ! pity it was that they thus courted danger
  By wishing to cross the frail structure that night,
"Twould better have been had each friend and each stranger
  Remained on the shore till the day brought the light :

Yes, pity it was that the train should have started
  'Mid the tempest's wild roar and horrible dun,
The Bridge might have stood and might never been parted
  Had prudence suggested the risk they would run.

But sad lamentations are all unavailing,
  "Tis done, and the ruin for ever is o'er ;
Dear life is extinct and sad hearts are bewailing
  The loss of the friends they may welcome no more.

We'll hide the dark picture, but deeply deplore it,
  And leave with their Maker those drowned in the tide,
He whose all-seeing eye was then watching o'er it,
  And Who on the wings of the whirlwind doth ride.

We'll hope that the friends who in death were then sleeping,
  Those who on that night found a watery grave,
Are all safe at home in the Father's kind keeping,
  Where tears never fall and no storms ever rave.

F

THE EIFFEL TOWER.

High up on the Eiffel Tower,
To lofty heights aspiring,
A swallow her nest
(So the papers attest)
Has built where she with her young may rest
Whenever they are tiring.

High up on the Eiffel Tower,
A charming situation,
There stretching away
To the far-distant bay,
The grand summer landscape ye survey
With happy contemplation.

High up on the Eiffel Tower,
Above the thronging people,
That from over the earth
To this land of mirth
All hasten as to their place of birth,
This land of spire and steeple.

High up on the Eiffel Tower,
An elevated station,
Earth's pageant and show
Far away down below,
Where Kings and Senators come and go,
And all the gay French nation.

High up on the Eiffel Tower,
Above the world's confusion,
Its clamour and noise,
And its low vulgar joys,
The merry laughter of girls and boys,
And nature's grand profusion.

High up on the Eiffel Tower,
Thy choice is much commended ;
Up over the trees
In the sweet cooling breeze,
Soaring, or resting, whene'er ye please
Pleasure with safety blended.

High up on the Eiffel Tower,
O ! safe and snug seclusion,
The worry and strife,
That for ever are rife,
On the earth, affect not there your life,
Ye fear not their intrusion.

High up on the Eiffel Tower—
Had I the wings or money,
Away I would soar,
To that not distant shore,
The wonders of Paris I'd explore,
And taste its milk and honey.

High up on the Eiffel Tower,
Who would not be a swallow ?
Selecting a site,
Where to sleep through the night,
And bask all day 'mid scenes of delight,
As they the insects follow.

High up on the Eiffel Tower :
O ! for a swallow's pinions,
To quit for a while,
With a rapturous smile,
This charmingly pleasant seagirt isle,
And see the French dominions.

High up on the Eiffel Tower,
Or down 'mid earth's green beauty,
Where flashes and glows,
As in silent repose,
The broad river through the landscape flows,
Rejoicing in its duty.

High up on the Eiffel Tower,
Or on the heaving ocean,
Whose depths so profound,
God's high praises resound,
As this terracqueous globe around,
It moves with varied motion.

High up on the Eiffel Tower,
Truth stranger is than fiction,
Who knows but I may
At some not distant day
Be priv'leged to cross the wat'ry way,
Some kind friend's benediction.

High up on the Eiffel Tower,
My wishes realising,
With grateful surprise,
Both the earth and the skies,
Above and below I cast my eyes,
The scene is so surprising.

High up on the Eiffel Tower,
The heavens bending o'er me,
Below earth's green vales,
Lofty hills and grand dales,
The far-reaching sea, with snow-white sails,
Lies stretching out before me.

High up on the Eiffel Tower,
Thence viewing the " gay city,"
Its parks and its squares,
With its alleys and lairs,
Where in poverty battling with cares
Dwell those whose lot we pity.

High up on the Eiffel Tower,
Watching the scene below me,
The myriads that throng
To this gay land of song,
Holding high carnival all day long,
Though none perhaps may know me.

High up on the Eiffel Tower,
I see the prancing horses,
Life's glitter and show,   ·
With its vice and its woe,
The peaceful streams that ripple and flow,
Along their winding courses.

High up on the Eiffel Tower,
My appetite appeasing,
At " Spiers and Pond,"
Or the cafés beyond,
Russian, or Flemish, or French so fond,
With anything that's pleasing.

High up on the Eiffel Tower,
And higher yet ascending,
A change greets the sight,
As from this giddy height,
The world I view with a strange delight,
While downwards my gaze bending.

High up on the Eiffel Tower,
Like flies upon the ceiling,
The people now seem
As below me they stream,
Life seems no more than an empty dream—
And all my senses reeling.

High up on the Eiffel Tower,
Earth's great ones not discerning,
In the crowds below
As they move to and fro,
Alike they come and alike they go,
And all for pleasure yearning.

High up on the Eiffel Tower,
Life's vain distinctions vanish,
The short and the tall,
Seem alike, all in all,
The rich and the poor, the great and small,
The English, French and Spanish.

High up on the Eiffel Tower,
Below me all is bustle,
Though where I am now,
On the Tower's very brow,
Earth's sounds reach me not I hear no row,
No faintest noise or rustle.

High up on the Eiffel Tower,
Absorbed in contemplation,
Some thoughts give me pain
As they flash through my brain,
While other please and fill me again
With joy and delectation.

High up on the Eiffel Tower,
What solid sure foundations
Must there underlie
This great building so high,
Which towers aloft 'twixt the earth and sky,
A wonder to the nations.

High up on the Eiffel Tower,
The world's great crowning wonder,
Old Time's with'ring hand,
'Twill resist and withstand,
Long ages hence it shall grace the land,
Defying e'en the thunder.

High up on the Eiffel Tower,
All honour to the Frenchman,
Whose wonderful skill,
Wrought with patience until
The building completed at his will,
Assisted by his henchmen.

High up on the Eiffel Tower,
I sing Eiffel's just praises,
Whose great mind conceived,
And whose skill hath achieved
A wonder that scarcely is believed,
As mankind on it gazes.

High up on the Eiffel Tower,
And as the structure rises,
O'er each meaner thing,
Of all buildings the king,
So too must he be whose praise I sing,
Whose work the world surprises.

High up on the Eiffel Tower,
Labour for pleasure changing,
If kind circumstance
Would allow me the chance
I would take a trip across to France,
'Mid joy unbounded ranging.

High up on the Eiffel Tower,
The giants both admiring
Both the Tower and the Man,
Whose wonderful plan,
Worked out in detail the nations scan.
With rapture never tiring.

High up on the Eiffel Tower,
O ! be the wish forgiven,
A glad song of praise
To my Maker I'd raise,
Whose goodness and mercy crown my days,
And gladden earth and heaven.

High up on the Eiffel Tower,
Sweet Angels condescending.
With us to converse,
And His glories rehearse,
In lofty strains of majestic verse,
Harmoniously blending.

High up on the Eiffel Tower,
As back through ages hoary,
From heaven there came,
Like a pure living flame,
Two noble spirits of deathless fame,
As reads the sacred story.

High up on the Eiffel Tower,
As on that mountain holy,
When bathed in the light,
There appeared to the sight,
Elias and Moses robed in white,
With Christ the meek and lowly.

High up on the Eiffel Tower,
Or in the depths below us,
On the land or the sea,
Where'er we may be,
The Angels are watching you and me,
And kind attentions show us.

High up on the Eiffel Tower,
Or in my chamber lonely,
It matters not where,
Since pure spirits are there,
Where bows the contrite heart in prayer,
And reverend worship only.

High up on the Eiffel Tower,
Nearer the heavens above us,
Where dwelling in light,
Never darkened by night,
Our dear departed withdrawn from sight,
Are living still and love us.

High up on the Eiffel Tower,
I thank thee little Swallow,
For pointing the way
To the regions of day,
Where each dear one that passes away
Beckons to us to follow.

High up on the Eiffel Tower,
Dear Lord we would adore Thee,
Our friends who have crossed,
Death's cold stream are not lost,
They have only joined Thy ransomed host
And worship now before Thee.

THE PENCIL.

To the Rev. C. L. Cameron.

———

DEAR SIR,

        Will you kindly permit me a word?
  The action I think will be fitting
That I should express to yourself, and no less
  To her who may by you be sitting —

My thanks for the pencil, the picture and pen,
  A "*Multum in parvo*" memento
Of your trip to France (which its worth does enhance)
  'Twas purchased with most kind intent O !

The present I prize, as most useful it is,
  Though not for this one reason only,
But that *you thought of me* when across the blue sea,
  Who sometimes am feeling most lonely.

And not only useful, 'tis pretty as well,
  In fact 'tis of art a small wonder ;
In it I can see tow'ring upwards so free
  A building that vies with the thunder.

I also behold to the right of the tower,
  A portrait of him the designer ;
Eiffel is his name, he is well known to fame,
  As those on the old plain of Shinar ;

Who sought in those far distant days to uprear
  (They seemed to believe they were able)
A building so high, it should reach to the sky,
  And be known as the "Tower of Babel."

I further perceive two balloons overhead,
  The cars swinging lightly below them,
And people are there, riding high in the air,
  I cannot say who, I don't know them.

I likewise observe other buildings around,
  A part of the French Exhibition ;
Of domes there are three and eight turrets I see,
  And *all* will admit definition

By those who have seen it, and those who can read
  The language in France that is spoken,
For clear to the view hangs a word picture too,
  Describing what it may betoken.

All this I behold in a picture so small,
  The head of a pin might conceal it,
Held up to the light, it shows well to the sight,
  Most clearly the day doth reveal it.

O ! how interesting the pencil to me,
  It is in itself quite a wonder,
A neat work of art 'tis unique in each part,
  The whole can be taken asunder,

Reversed, and screwed in and then used as a pen,
  A clever and rare combination,
With lead or with ink I can write what I think,
  When musing in sweet meditation.

Then, Sir, once again, I will thank you and her,
  It cannot be other than fitting,
That I should *first use* and devote to the muse
  While here in my quiet room sitting—

The pencil and pen you so kindly gave me,
  And miniature picture within it :
A *souvenir to me*, brought from over the sea,
  Though nought have I done that could win it.

In the years that may come I the gift shall esteem,
  And ever think kindly of you, Sir,
Who when far away *thought of me* on that day
  As no doubt your Lady did too, Sir.

  Sept., 1889.

A SOLITARY SWALLOW.

November 24th, 1888.

Ah ! whence thou little wingëd stranger—
  Whence comest thou this dark November day ?
Where hast thou been, thou airial ranger,
  Come, tell us why thou dost prolong thy stay ?

Thy friends long since have all departed
  Across the sea to distant sunny climes,
They plumed their pinions ere they started,
  And sweetly twittered their love many times.

We watched them as they flocked together
  Day after day until they took their flight,
Warned by the approaching wintry weather,
  To seek a home more genial and more bright.

But why thou little forlorn creature,
  Why art thou battling with the raging wind ?
Admonished by the unerring teacher,
  Thy friends have left these wintry shores behind.

Why is it thou art here abiding,
  A lonely swallow in a wintry sky ?
On thy outstretched wings serenely riding,
  Though none of all thy kith or kin be nigh.

Did they for some offence proclaim thee—
   Turn thee adrift to wander here alone ;
Or did they in bird language *name* thee,
   And make thee for thy venial faults atone ?

Or did'st thou on that autumn morning,
   When all thy feathery tribe spread wings for flight,
Did'st thou regardless of their warning,
   Prolong the drowsy slumbers of the night ?

And when at length thou did'st awaken
   From out thy peaceful, long protracted sleep,
And did'st discover that thou wast forsaken,
   Did'st thou, sweet birdie, in thy anguish weep ?

Or wast thou sick and unattended,
   And left alone to languish, droop and die :
And did'st thou struggle on though unbefriended,
   And yet recover though no help was nigh ?

Then mounting upwards on thy pinions,
   Desiring much thy new-found strength to try,
And longing for thy lost companions,
   Whom now thou seekest through the earth and sky.

But still unable (not discerning
   What guides unerring the vast multitude),
To trace thy way, though strongly yearning,
   For friendship's joys amid thy solitude.

Yes, all unable, instinct failing,
   To guide thee *singly* as it guides the *throng*,
Thy weary flights all unavailing
   To reach the distant land of light and song.

Was this, or that, or what the reason,
   That thou art left to linger here to-day ?
A poor wee thing quite out of season,
   Thy friends and kindred all so far away

Whate'er the cause of thy remaining
   In this inclement, cold and wint'ry clime,
Though past our efforts at explaining,
   In stately verse or simple tinkling rhyme :

We yet are glad to have thee near us,
  Reminding us of brighter, bygone days,
When sun and flowers conspired to cheer us,
  And all the woods rang out with notes of praise.

When birds their harmonies descanting,
  All jubilant with joy among the trees,
And nature everywhere enchanting,
  Delightful odours borne on every breeze.

Yes, we rejoice that you remainest,
  Recalling to us those glad summer hours,
And hope that though alone thou reignest,
  Some pleasure may be thine as well as our's;

Though much we fear a form so slender
  Will not endure the winter's frost and snow,
Thy nature frail, and all alas ! too tender,
  Thy stay we fear will work thee nought but woe.

We, therefore, to avoid thee anguish,
  Urge thee at once this wintry land to fly ;
We should be grieved to see thee languish,
  And pine and droop and prematurely die.

Then hasten birdie, quit these regions,
  Go, wing thy way to yonder golden shore,
And there among those feath'ry legions,
  Again unite with all thy friends of yore.

THE FIRST SWALLOW.

April 22nd, 1889.

Ah ! dear little swallow, we welcome thee back,
  We all are delighted to see thee return,
Thy presence gives birth to a feeling of mirth,
  The summer's approach we now clearly discern.

From hesperian climes, and over the sea,
  Thy wings and the breezes have brought thee again ;
From that distant strand to our dear native land,
  Thou traversed the turbulent wide rolling main.

But how did'st thou manage, my sweet little bird,
  When gathered around thee the darkness of night,
Far out on the sea, O ! what shelter can be,
  To screen and protect such a wee little mite ?

Perchance on the rigging of some passing ship,
  Or perched up aloft on the towering mast,
In the lap of the deep rocked safely asleep,
  Unheeding the rage of the storms as they passed,

In their grandeur and might and deafening roar
  The skies all enveloped in blackness and gloom,
The lightning's wild flash, and the thunder's loud crash,
  That seemed in their fury to threaten thy doom.

But all unconcerned firmly clutching the rope,
  Thy little head sunk in the down on thy breast,
Rocked calmly asleep in the lap of the deep,
  Refreshing, restoring and soothing thy rest.

The morning now shines and my birdie awakes,
  The storms have departed, the skies are all clear,
And stretching away in the light of the day,
  The shores of old England distinctly appear.

Ah ! dear little bird thou art constant and kind,
  Although thou dost leave us when winter appears :
'Tis only because the beneficent laws
  That govern thy nature and number thy years

Forbid thee remaining in this wintry land ;
  It's rigours by far are too searching for thee,
The frost and the snow, and the piercing winds' blow,
  Thou can'st not endure ; therefore over the sea

To a sunnier shore and more genial clime,
  For a brief little while thou wingest thy way ;
Then back with the spring on thy lightsome glad wing
  Delighted thou comest to linger and stay.

But where are thy comrades, remaining behind?
   Or did'st thou outstrip them in swiftness of flight?
So eager to see thy old friends, and to be
   The first little swallow to gladden our sight;

And thy feathery kindred's arrival announce—
   "They're all on the wing, and will shortly be here,"
Like angels of light they will burst on our sight,
   And we all shall rejoice to see them appear.

O! yes—one, two, three, quite a host I can see,
   All pitching and soaring and floating along,
So glad to be here with their presence to cheer,
   And sweetly to twitter their little love-song.

Sweet heralds of mercy, harbingers of joy,
   Precursors of pleasure! glad tidings ye bring;
Hope kindles anew as in heaven's clear blue
   Again we behold the companions of spring.

Since last ye were here, O! what changes have been!
   How many dear precious and loved ones are gone!
Kindhearted and true they have passed from our view,
   In the darkness of night or glimmering dawn;

Or during the day we have seen them depart,
   In sorrow and sadness have whispered "good bye!"
Like ye, they have fled, and we thought they were dead,
   But they only have gone to a sunnier sky.

Escaping like ye the cold pitiless blast,
   And all the stern rigours of life's wintry day,
Its frost and its snow, or its anguish and woe,
   All, all they have left far behind and away.

And though (unlike ye) they can never return,
   To gladden our hearts with their presence again,
Our pleasures to share or our troubles help bear,
   When round us shall gather misfortune and pain;

Yet we hope and believe when the winter is past,
   The winter of life with its shadows and gloom
Shall fade to the spring with the joys it will bring,
   'Mid heaven's green beauty and glad vernal bloom.

We shall see our old friends and know them again,
  As we now do behold and recognize you,
On yon' heavenly plains where joy ever reigns,
  The friendships of earth we again shall renew.

THE VOICE OF THE CUCKOO.

'Tis the spring of the year and the Cuckoo is here,
  His voice we have heard many times,
And his form we have seen as he floated between
  The firs and yon low-bending limes.

To this isle of the sea every year cometh he,
  He comes as the voice of the spring,
From his soft mellow throat his peculiar note
  He utters e'en while on the wing.

When fair April appears smiling sweet thro' her tears,
  And soft vernal breezes do blow,
There then breaks on the ear as from some other sphere
  The sound that enraptures us so.

How delighted we heard this most wonderful bird,
  In years that have long passed away,
And we listen once more as in those days of yore
  To what this strange bird has to say.

And though ever the same, crying only its name,
  It yet has a charm all its own,
Since it tells many things both to peasants and kings
  Which otherwise might not be known.

O ! then what does it say as it sits on yon spray,
  Of what to mankind does it tell,
As it utters its note from the depths of its throat
  And casts over all its strange spell ?

It reveals hidden truths both to maidens and youths,
  And whispers sweet peace to old age ;
By *suggestion* it brings to the mind many things
  Life's sorrows to heal or assuage.

It inspires us with hope when in darkness we grope,
  And tells of a spring yet to be,
That for ever shall last compensating all past
  When all shall be happy and free.

To the well-attuned ear in its notes soft and clear,
  Sweet voices seem on us to call,
And they tell of a clime far away beyond time
  To which nature beckons us all.

But 'tis now " leafy June," when he sings his last tune,
  And ends here his all too brief stay,
Far away then he flies to some other fair skies
  And others to charm with his lay.

THE SUNSHINE AT LAST.

At length while the birds in full chorus are singing,
Old Sol his glad beams o'er the landscape is flinging
  And pouring his splendours on hill, dale and plain,
Infusing new life and imparting fresh beauty,
Inviting the husbandman forth to his duty
  And cheering the heart of each labouring swain.

No longer is heard discontented repining,
The clouds have departed, the bright sun is shining,
  Old nature rejoices and mortals are glad ;
Light laughter and joy now succeed the depression
That reigned all around like an evil obsession,
  The season will not after all be so bad.

The hay crops have suffer'd, 'tis true, but the reason
Is not *altogether* the fault of the season,
  'Tis *partly* the want of *more patience* in man ;
" All things come to him " oft 'tis said " who by waiting "
Receives in due time what his faith contemplating,
  And what shall reward his most sensible plan.

Grass should not be cut till the farmer knows whether,
Unsettled, or fixed, foul or fair is the weather,
  And Science this matter can surely divine ;
By noting the sky in the evening and morning
We take nature's blessing or otherwise warning,
  The clouds will give rain or the grand sun will shine.

Too much rain for the hay, but (and O ! what a blessing).
The root crops will thrive, much enriched by the dressing,
  The cereals, too, 'twill fill out and improve ;
The cattle will thus with ourselves who confided,
Have food in abundance by nature provided,
  When slow vegetation shall tardily move.

We thus clearly see that a kind compensation
Through nature doth run for the good of the nation,
  Though prone to complain and short-sighted are we ;
We still will believe that o'er all is presiding
Wisdom wedded with power the universe guiding,
  Controlling the forces that round us we see.

    August, 1890.

THE SWALLOWS PREPARING FOR FLIGHT.

Away o'er the waters the Swallows are going,
See ! see ! what a host of white pinions are showing,
  And oh ! how they flutter and flap as they sit ;
Each morning assembled in grave consultation,
Discussing their prospects with much animation,
  They wondrously talkative seem as they twitt.

They swarm on the housetops, they flit and they flutter,
And sounds full of meaning continually utter,
  Indeed, 'tis the *language* these birds speak and know ;
Their object no doubt in thus meeting together,
Has some sort of ref'rence to wind and to weather,
  And who shall be leader and when they shall go.

'Tis pleasant to watch them thus all in commotion
Just prior to taking their flight o'er the ocean,
  And notice how loving these creatures all seem ;
What sweet intercourse, how each looks at the other,
With all the affection of sister and brother,
  And all the devotion of love's early dream.

A few days at most and they all will be leaving,
Withdrawing their presence, our country bereaving,
  And winging their way to more genial climes,
Where food supplies plentiful, insects abundant,
In hot summer lands always strangely fecundent,
  Supply to demand overdone many times.

Already they stretch out their wings as if testing
Their strength for the journey which may have no resting,
  Until they arrive on the sea's farther shore ;
Who knows but to-day they their flight may be taking,
The exodus they have been long contemplating,
  To-morrow may dawn and we view them no more.

G 2

Farewell, feather'd friends, then, but O ! not for ever,
Although time and space intervene and us sever
  We hope to behold you again before long ;
When winter is past and its dreariness over,
The springtime returns and the lark from the clover
  Ascends to the skies with its worship of song.

Till then we will wait with a sense of our duty,
Till earth once again shall enrobe in her beauty
  And ye happy birds to these islands return ;
Bringing back on your wings from over the waters
Both healing and health to our sons and our daughters,
  And comfort to those who for absent ones yearn.

'Tis thus we look forward, our hearts strangely yearning,
To that happy time when our lost ones returning,
  Or rather when we shall rejoin them elsewhere ;
Life's winter behind and its summer before us,
The darkness all past and the light breaking o'er us
  And sweetest tranquility follow earth's care.

      October, 1890.

TO MRS. W. MOORE, OF WHITLEY, READING.

October 10th, 1889.

This pond'rous globe once more its circuit hath completed.
  Around the central orb 'mid other rolling spheres :
And Madam, once again thy birthday is repeated
  And thus another unit added to thy years.

This the auspicious day when first the light revealing
    That breaks from yonder skies upon the darkened earth,
Into thy chamber crept and on thy eyeballs stealing
    Around thee shed a halo at thy very birth.

To thee this Autumn day all other days excelling,
    No day to equal this the calender contains ;
Within thy mother's heart what joy beyond the telling,
    When reaping the reward of all her fears and pains.

Yes, on this happy day thy earthly race thou started,
    Beneath no doubt, benign, and kind celestial fires ;
Which ever from the skies upon mankind have darted
    Their influence.   (So taught our Astrologic sires).

To thee, I trust, the gods have ever been propitious,
    Scatt'ring their blessings all along thy pilgrim way ;
That still on thee they smile and ne'er prove aught capricious,
    That still upon thy path heaven's cheering sunbeams play :

That ever in thy home and on thy spreading table,
    The " horn of plenty " daily pours its rich supplies ;
That everything beneath thy sloping roof's broad gable,
    Inspire the thankful heart and gladden well the eyes.

That peace and calm content are ever there abounding,
    The voice of prayer and praise uplifted every day,
In gratitude to Him the song of thanks resounding,
    Whose goodness crowns our lives, Whose counsel guides
      our way.

That health and strength thy comely, robust form possessing,
    And circulating well in all thy purple veins,
(Health is, of all good things life's richest, choicest blessing,
    No treasure equals this, immunity from pains.)

That troops of loving friends throng ever round and near thee,
    Their purposes with thine in mutual concord blend ;
That circumstances all conspire alike to cheer thee,
    O ! may thy pleasure last and never have an end.

That he thy Consort, too, upon thee ever doting
    (Each bound to each by ties, unbroken, strong and sure),
May ever prove most true, his all to thee devoting,
    No evanescent love, but *lasting*, deep and pure.

Love linked in purest love and heart to heart united,
  Through life thus trav'lling on no sorrows may ye know,
Affection thus betrothed and ever firmly plighted,
  Is Paradise on earth ; celestial bliss below.

Each one the other's wants in love anticipating,
  And vying each with each in blissful conflict there :
Heaven's happiness supreme ye thus are antedating,
  The joys the Angels know ye thus already share.

Then, Madam, please herewith, permit me just to offer
  To thee my heart's best wish upon this happy day,
While my poor feeble muse its services would proffer,
  And in thy presence now, would this small tribute lay.

———

While sincerely hoping that the blessings described in
the foregoing verses have ever been and will ever *continue*
to be enjoyed to the full by your worthy self, I have yet
provided for all possible contingencies by adding what
immediately follows :—

ADDENDUM.

But *should* thy tranquil skies by clouds be ever darkened
  (As clouds sometimes will mar and blot the fairest day),
O ! then restrain thy grief ; be not too much disheartened,
  No more than thou can'st bear upon thee will He lay.

How oft the troubles that we think look dark before us,
  And fill our dreading minds with long foreboding fear,
Like threat'ning thunderclouds but harmlessly burst o'er us,
  The *storm goes rushing by*, again the skies are clear.

Or like the murky fog the atmosphere pervading,
  Obstructing heaven's clear light and blotting out the day,
Earth's fair enchanting scenes from mortal sight are fading,
  And *on our very path most thick* it seems to lay.

But as we journey on, our pathway firmly treading,
  What looked so dark and drear gets brighter as we go ;
The fog at our approach, which all around was spreading,
  Now modestly retires, and fainter seems to grow.

'Tis thus with troubles seen when in the distance looming ;
    Alarmed at what we see ('tis magnified by fear),
More frightened still we grow, such ugly forms assuming,
    Our fancy gives them shapes they never have when near.

Then let us live to day nor fear about the morrow,
    But put our trust in Him Who rules the raging sea,
All anxious thoughts dismiss which cause us needless sorrow,
    "Too good to be unkind ; too wise to err is He."

On this thy natal day, O ! Madam, be not fearful,
    And give no place to that which thou may'st never see ;
Let faith sustain thy heart, and ever be thou cheerful ;
    "Our times are in His hands."   Let this thought solace
       thee.

He notes the Sparrow fall ; our very hairs He numbers,
    The red-winged lightnings too are under His control,
He guides the comet's course ; His voice it is that thunders ;
    The universe the frame of which He is the soul.

To His most dutiful, obedient sons and daughters,
    "The promises of God, are all ' Amen ' and ' Yea,' "
Conspicuous this :—"When thou passest through the waters,
    "They shall not o'erflow thee ; though much they surge
      and sway."

"When walking through the fire, however fierce its raging,
    "The flames shall not ascend to do thee aught of harm ;
"My presence there shall be, its fury all assuaging,
    "Composing all thy fears ; protecting from alarm.

"When all is dark around, no faintest ray to cheer thee,
    "Put thou thy hand in Mine and I will lead the way,
"Although thou can'st not see, *believe* that I am near thee,
    "And soon the darkest night shall end in brightest day."

Then let us trust the word which our dear Lord hath spoken,
    His Word more lasting is than heaven's strong pillars are ;
He is the Truth itself which never can be broken,
    Though sink in depths of night, sun, moon and every star.

Our strength and refuge He, always in Him confiding,
    Though mountains from their seats should leap into the sea
Though Nature be convulsed ; securely there abiding
    We need not ever fear, since Nature's God is He.

TO MY MOTHER

On attaining the age of Sixty Years, October 5th, 1877.

Dearest Mother in these verses,
   Which I now present to thee,
Feebly my poor muse rehearses,
   Fragments of thy history ;
Just recounts in simple measure,
   Doings of the fleeting past,
Hoping it will give thee pleasure,
   (May thy joys for ever last),
Please accept these lines I pray,
   Written for thy natal day.

Three-score years have pass'd before thee,
   Seared with age is now thy brow ;
Time has rolled its billows o'er thee,
   We can trace their impress now ;
Wrinkles on thy face are showing,
   Dimness settles on thine eyes,
That in days of yore were glowing
   Brightly as the morning skies ;
In thy hair are streaks of grey,
   Proofs of nature's sad decay.

Childhood's days are gone for ever,
   Youthful vigour is no more,
Death thy life may shortly sever
   And thy pilgrimage be o'er ;
Sickness often has o'erta'en thee,
   Brought thee down and laid thee low,
There in weakness to detain thee
   In the depths of grief and woe,
Holding thee a pris'ner there,
   Causing us much anxious care.

Often we have seen thee lying
  Pale and sickly on thy bed,
Fearing life's poor flame was dying
  As the rapid moments fled.
But as on thy features gazing
  We beheld a change appear,
Joy at once our spirits raising,
  Danger pass'd and with it fear,
Hope nigh smother'd in the breast
  Now revived her drooping crest.

Thus is lengthen'd thy probation,
  And we have thee with us still,
Daily filling thy vocation
  With a cheerful mind and will;
Health and strength again returning,
  Bringing back the joy that we
Had foregone when sadly learning
  Of the pangs oppressing thee:
We thy happiness now share,
  Gladly cast aside our care.

Thou hast lived to see around thee
  Sons grown up to manhood's prime,
And their offspring, too, surround thee,
  Telling of the flight of time.
When thou art the past reviewing—
  Early days and riper years—
All thy griefs and joys renewing,
  All thy hopes and all thy fears;
Mingled feelings fill thy mind,
  Joy and gratitude combined.

Thou hast had thy share of sadness,
  Felt at times the lash of pain,
And thou hast had days of gladness,
  As the sunshine follows rain.
Oh! how chequer'd and how changing
  Is our pathway here below,
Now, 'mid joys ecstatic ranging,
  Now, where sorrow's teardrops flow,
Fluctuating all appears,
  Passing through this vale of tears.

Memory now, with great precision,
  (Oh ! how wondrous is her power !)
Brings before the mental vision
  Almost every by-gone hour,
All the past at once restoring
  Childhood's early days and years ;
When distress'd, thy aid imploring,
  Mute and silent in our tears,
Readily thou would'st impart
  Consolation to the heart.

And thy children each remember
  How thy presence did them cheer
In the dreary, dark December,
  And through all the changing year.
At all times their lives inspiring
  With thy kindly word and smile,
Ever patient, never tiring,
  Free from all deceit and guile,
Ever gladly thy love show,
  Round them thy protection throw.

When affliction's piercing anguish
  Ever did their heart-strings thrill,
Thou would'st sigh to see them languish.
  And thine eyes with tears would fill,
With much care their wants attending,
  All their needs thou would'st supply ;
Anxious o'er their couches bending
  With love's ever-watchful eye,
Till disease and aching pain
  Fled and health returned again.

May thy time be here extended
  Even yet for many years,
And when life's career is ended
  May you from this vale of tears
To that region be translated
  Where it is eternal spring :
And where Saints with joy elated,
  Songs and hallelujahs sing.
There with those white-robed ones dwell,
  Whose pure joys no tongue can tell.

May thy children, too, and Consort
   Mingle with the heavenly throng,
Join to swell the blissful concert,
   Roll the pleasing notes along ;
There together dwell for ever,
   When life's fleeting days are o'er,
Where death never shall us sever,
   Sorrows shall oppress no more.
May thy family complete
   Meet around that glorious seat.

REMINISCENCES OF HOME.

A Letter in verse to an elder Brother.

DEAR BROTHER,

   You told me that if I would write
And send you a line now and then,
You'd gladly reply. So I want to know why
   It is, that your ink and your pen,

Or possibly pencil (I do not care which)
   Lie idle the table upon,
While each morning I wait the click of the gate
   So eager your letter to con.

Each morning I look for the postman to bring
   A letter dear Brother from you ;
The neat little square telling how you all fare,
   Your children, yourself, and wife too.

And whether my letter you duly received,
   And if you the paper have found,
The " *Hampshire Gazette*," where my verses are set,
   Of which you informed me a sound

Had reach'd you; that some one a paper had sent
  They did not quite know whence or where,
But thought from the name that most likely it came
  From over the sea; somewhere there.

Yes, over the sea, where the little birds went,
  Of which in my verses I sing,
The Swallows that flew, o'er the waters so blue
  And come back again in the spring.

Excepting, of course, the poor thing that was left
  To soar in a bleak wintry sky,
To wander alone and its sad fate to moan
  Then finally languish and die.

But what am I thinking of, writing of birds?
  My muse has gone surely astray:
What I meant to do was to just remind you
  Of promises made on that day,

When at Norwood we met, we four Brother boys,
  To pay our respect to the dead,
Our love to him show amid sorrow and woe
  For him who toil'd hard for our bread.

Yes, him, our dear Father, who all the day long
  And sometimes all through the still night,
While other men slept to his work closely kept
  And toil'd till the morning's glad light

Broke over the earth, flooding hill, dale and plain,
  And cheering the palace and cot,
And no man could be more contented than he
  Or grumble less over his lot.

For do we not know how he whistled and sang
  When things would go smoothly and well,
And when they did not he would still bear his lot
  With patience I need not now tell.

Ah! yes, we remember the humour and fun
  To which he would sometimes give play,
The time to beguile and to make us boys smile
  And dull carking care drive away.

How sometimes his harmless and innocent jokes
  Would cause quite a ripple to flow,
As from morning till night he worked with his might
  With Bill, Ted and Harry and Joe,

Who all worked at home in the years that are past
  With Father, so healthy and strong,
Who hamm'ring away at the leather all day
  Would sometimes break forth into song

In which we all join'd with a hearty goodwill,
  He taking the *bass* as you know,
While we at his side sang the *treble* with pride
  And thus did the merry hours flow.

And O ! how we worked all in harmony then
  And how the old cottage did ring ;
As loudly and long we continued our song,
  Right lustily did we all sing.

Sure never was Conqueror, Statesman, or King,
  More happy than then we all were
When through the glad days we all sang hymns of praise
  And Father sometimes knelt in prayer

Imploring His mercy, beseeching His grace,
  Desiring His goodness to know,
And longing to feel what the Lord might reveal
  When He should His blessing bestow.

The awl and the bristles we then did apply
  And merrily all stitched away,
All motion and swing as in concert we sing,
  While neighbours would listen and say

" What very nice voices these boys have all got
  " And O ! how the father can sing,
" How happy they are, not a string that does jar,
  "Their voices in harmony ring."

And happy we were, poor old Dad and we boys,
  In those good old days that are past,
How we pulled the threads thro' and how the wax flew
  And how Father stuck to the " last."

Yes, stuck to the last upon which he would fix
  With wondrous precision and care,
The uppers that we, Harry, you, Ted and me
  In closing had each had a share.

With pincers adapted he deftly would pull
  The upper well down at the toe,
Then turn to the heel and examine and feel—
  He'd have it exact as you know.

Then placing the block on his broad ample knees
  (How wondrously hard those knees were),
He'd nail it quite fast with his tacks to the last
  And thus for the sewing prepare.

With strong waxen threads then together he'd bind,
  While down him large sweat drops would roll,
As round it the welt he would sew like a belt
  Connecting the two with the sole.

Ah ! yes, with strong hemp all well twisted and spun,
  Like that with which Samson was bound,
His shoes he would sew from the heel to the toe
  The toe to the heel and all round.

Yes, start from the heel and go round by the toe,
  Then back to the heel as the goal,
And then (dear old man) he would sew on the ran'
  And double it down to the sole.

And then he the bottom at once would fill in,
  Nor paper nor rubbish he'd use,
But old harness strips and good stout leather chips
  With these would he fill in his shoes.

Each piece fitted in and all well pasted down,
  A solid foundation thus laid,
Both firmly and neat thus insuring the feet
  From any discomfort when made.

Then well hamm'ring out until quite tough and strong,
  Again the large sweat drops would roll,
The floor would quite shake and the walls seem to quake
  While Father thus hammer'd the sole.

Ah ! poor dear old man what a number of soles,
   With labour and patience and care
Has he hammer'd out and well batter'd about
   For frail human bodies to wear.

This thick outer-sole thus made ready for use,
   Prepared by a series of blows,
Forthwith he makes fast to the in-sole and last
   And thus 'tis the shoe shapes and grows.

Then trimming it neatly and closely all round
   And making a channel or groove,
Where concealed from the eye the stitches might lie
   And from their snug bed never move.

This groove he would make with the point of his knife,
   Quite close to the edge of the sole,
Then open it wide with a tool at his side
   Resembling a punt-hook and pole.

The threadmaking process he now would begin
   The strong hempen cords as before,
Of sixteen small strands twisted well with his hands,
   Sometimes he would have less or more ;

Depending, of course, on the hemp that he used,
   Unless it should chance to be flax,
Which sometimes it would, and *that* ever was good
   And always he'd have the best wax

Through which he the well-twisted threads would now draw,
   Until they would shine bright as gold.
The use of the wax on the hemp or the flax
   The threads all together 'twould hold,

And make them endure and not ever give way
   But hold the work well in its place,
When the wearer should go or plough'd fields to sow
   As sometimes it chanced was the case.

For sometimes men came from the villages near,
   And to him their money they paid,
The ploughman well knew where to get a strong shoe,
   Both soundly and honestly made.

And then he the points of the thread would prepare,
  Both waxing and twisting them well,
Then fasten with care the stout bristle or hair
  They get from the wild hog and sell.

And now the hard labour again would begin,
  Again the large sweat drops would roll,
As with might and with main he'd stitch, pull and strain
  While sewing this thick outer-sole.

From the heel to the toe, the toe to the heel,
  As when he the shoe first began,
When round it the welt he had sewn like a belt
  And round the heel also the ran'.

So now : every stitch being tightly drawn in,
  His thread round the hammer he'd wind,
Or otherwise twist round his hand or his wrist
  And on the old handleather bind.

The stitches embedded well down in the sole,
  The channel again he would close,
And quite out of sight buried neatly and light
  They snugly and calmly repose.

The lift and the top-piece attention now claim,
  The pieces that make up the heel,
The first he would sew while the other you know
  He'd rivet and well mount with steel.

Then round with the pane of his hammer he'd go,
  And batter the edges well in,
Then shave it all round and thus make the heel sound
  Then toss the boot up with a spin

And turn it about and examine it well
  As often you know he would do ;
By this means he saw each defect and each flaw
  That marr'd the yet unfinished shoe.

These flaws and defects he at once would remove,
  The remedy he would apply,
More shapely would grow both the heel and the toe
  When scann'd by his well practised eye.

The scraping and rubbing and polishing then
   His energies next would employ,
The " long-stick " he'd use on the soles of the shoes
   And quickly their colour destroy ;

Or rather their colour change into a glow,
   A glow that would glisten and shine,
His face 'twould reflect and no spot could detect,
   So brilliant the polish and fine.

Ah ! yes, and no wonder, so hard would he rub,
   That all round about him would shake,
The tools and the crocks, and his own raven locks
   Like aspen leaves quiver and quake.

The tip on the toe he then firmly would fix,
   Like that he had placed on the heel ;
Nor cast iron nor wrought wearing quickly to nought
   But both made of well hardened steel.

And now on the well polished surface he draws
   The lines where the nails are to go,
The stout sewing awl seemed to suit best of all
   He used this most frequent you know.

These lines he would make so exact and precise,
   He used neither measure nor rule,
But simply rely on his well practised eye
   Which guided unerring the tool.

Lines four, five, or six, as the case chanced to be,
   Each parallel running with each,
Narrow up at the toe then wider they grow
   And down to the waist they would reach.

Now all being ready he hammers away,
   The nailing forthwith he begins,
The shoe bindeth he with a strap to his knee
   Which crosses just down by his shins.

The nails he would take from a tin or a bowl,
   And shoot in the palm of his hand,
Where sometimes a score or perhaps even more
   He would hold.   The bowl he would stand

H

Back on the seat.   At once then his hammer he'd take,
  And grasping it firmly and fast,
A nail gently drops, from the palm to the tops
  Of his fingers.   Wrought iron or cast ;

Which, held by the hand he the point presses in,
  Still holding with finger and thumb,
First lightly, tip tap, then a smart heavy rap
  At once on the hob-nail would come,

Which drives it well in, and another one then,
  He places direct by its side,
The nails drop and fall to his fingers till all
  Are driven where they must abide.

Thus row after row all round-headed or square,
  In rapid succession appear,
The hammer flies fast while at intervals past
  A nail whizzes close to the ear

And strikes on the wall like a shot or a shell,
  Though happily does not explode,
And sometimes we'd say "That's right, Dad, fire away,"
  And sometimes we'd say "Well, I'm blow'd."

Thus whirring and whizzing, the nails disappear,
  All driven well into the sole,
Excepting the few that escaped from the shoe
  And flew to the north or south pole.

By which I but mean to the right or the left
  Of the room in which we then were,
The north or south wall, simply this, that is all,
  I meant nothing more, I declare.

Thus the nailing goes on till all are complete,
  Each row in the neatly drawn lines,
All even and true, much improving the shoe
  With elegance strength now combines.

No longer now needed the last-hook he takes
  And hooking it firmly and fast,
Without more ado at once draws from the shoe
  The much-abused, well-batter'd last.

A hole near the top, made on purpose, of course,
    In which he his hook might insert,
Then a long pull and strong, a strong pull and long
    And always escaping unhurt.

Yes, happily, always escaping unhurt,
    While drawing the last as you knew,
On which he had laid the foundation and made
    With self-satisfaction, the shoe.

Sometimes he the hook in his right hand would take,
    His left he would place on the heel,
Then tug, pull and strain, with his might and his main
    Until he a motion could feel,

When out with a jerk all at once it would come,
    The last which he put in the first
Or rather *on* which he would fix what we stitch.
    In stitching us boys were well versed.

Not always, however, the last would thus come,
    Howe'er he might tug with his steel,
Howe'er he might strain all at times would be vain,
    No motion the last would reveal.

When this was the case (and it often would be),
    Fresh means he would have to employ
The last to eject (and the inside inspect)
    And all its resistance destroy.

The shoe, therefore, now he would turn upside down,
    The hook-handle place 'neath his feet,
The toe and the heel he would grapple like steel
    And slightly would rise from his seat.

His strong brawny hands grasp the shoe in their might,
    At once it is certain and plain,
As firmly he grips both the heel and toe tips
    That further resistance is vain.

His head bowing low and his arms reaching down
    (The hook-handle still 'neath his feet)
His whole strength he'd bring and the last would outfling
    And make its ejectment complete.

H 2

Now the edge of the sole, the heel to the toe,
   The toe to the heel once again,
He rubs with a cloth which defies both the moth
   And all its destructive fell train.

This cloth he would twist and bind well on his thumb
   And then the saliva would fall,
With which he would dub and with which he would rub
   The edges, the hardest of all.

So hard would he rub that he often would wear
   The cloth into shreds or a hole,
The tools would quite shake and again the crocks quake
   And once more the sweats drops would roll.

Then placing the shoe in a dry, airy place,
   Sometimes on the old window sill,
Or down on the floor where the sunshine would pour
   And stream through the window until

The dampness exhaled ; the shoe then would be fit
   For inking and " finishing off,"
When Dad strikes a match and the fumes our throats catch
   Producing a sneeze or a cough.

Yes, Dad strikes a match and the candle he lights,
   The irons he heats in the flame,
Which now pips and pops while the fat drips and drops
   The irons being chiefly to blame.

They hang o'er the flame that it cannot ascend,
   The smoke seems to wreathe and to curl,
Around the iron plays, seeming all in a maze,
   And all in a swim and a swirl.

While thus they are heating the heelball he takes,
   Which always, you know, would be hard,
To stand well the test and to wear like the rest
   The soft ones he'd always discard.

The heelball he takes 'tween his finger and thumb,
   This also he holds to the fire.
Both frequent and oft thus to make it more soft
   And pliant as he may desire.

On the edge of the sole, the heel to the toe,
   The toe right away to the heel,
This compo he dubs and with energy rubs
   Excepting, of course, the bright steel.

The iron then he takes, black as soot with the smoke,
   And wipes it all round with a cloth,
A cloth kept close by which though black always dry
   And never infested by moth.

Then lightly his well-wetted tongue would he touch
   And instantly on the iron press,
By this means he knew if the iron was hot through,
   At least would conjecture or guess.

For if the wet clung then the tool was but warm,
   But if it flew off it was hot,
'Twould splutter and phiz and rush off with a whizz,
   Which otherwise surely 'twould not.

And thus with his finger and thumb he would test
   And always the heat ascertain,
Nor ever would use on the boots or the shoes
   The tool when 'twas labour in vain.

But always would have the iron heated exact,
   According to this simple rule,
Which when it was done round the sole he would run
   With pleasure the well heated tool.

The heel and the toe and the neat sloping waist,
   As also the broad ample tread,
Each part in its turn for the iron seemed to yearn
   As anxious the heelball to spread.

And this it would do, press and work it well in,
   Imparting a gloss and a glow,
The edges would shine like the coal in the mine
   The tread, waist, the heel and the toe.

A rub with the cloth and the shoes are complete,
   Excepting a few trifling things,
As blocking the fronts (with a few parting grunts)
   And lastly supplying the strings.

Then off to the wearer with pleasure he takes
    The shoes, which he knows are well made,
Both neatly and strong and will sure to last long,
    No better produced by the Trade.

No remorse does he feel as the money he takes,
    His conscience is clear as the sun,
He knows they will bear close inspection, and wear
    At least while full thirteen moons run.*

Ah ! poor dear old man, like a dream it all seems,
    That flies the approach of the morn,
But a short while ago us Brothers you know
    In sorrow were shapen and born.

Then, Father was young, he was healthy and strong,
    And just in his beauty and prime,
With Mother, his bride, full of courage and pride
    They felt not the burden of time.

But years rolled along and us boys grew to men,
    And Father's black locks turn'd to grey,
Poor Mother appears bow'd with weakness and years
    And first of the two pass'd away.

But Father yet linger'd a brief little while,
    His footsteps were failing and slow,
And shortly he, too, was withdrawn from our view
    His work he had done and must go.

Yes, Father and Mother have both pass'd away,
    Life's brief earthly race they have run,
Its sorrow and care now no longer they share
    Their work is completed and done.

Poor Walter and John too, alas ! are no more,
    And Benjamin died long ago ;
Yes, dear little Ben, a mere baby boy when
    He left the world's sorrow and woe.

And now there remain but us four Brother boys
    And one only Sister is left,
All dwelling apart, but I trust one in heart,
    As equally all are bereft.

---

* He always warranted his boots to wear twelve calendar months.

Our own wives and children we now must attend,
  And Lizzie her husband and boy,
Who all of us wish (and *most heartily* wish)
  The greatest contentment and joy.

But O ! how erratic my muse has become,
  How far it has led me astray
From what I first meant, when my only intent
  A few simple words was to say.

I hope you are well and enjoying good health,
  As also your partner and wife,
The girls and the boys with their dolls and their toys
  With pleasure and happiness rife.

The kind invitation extended to me
  Old Chatham's Dockyards to inspect,
If kind circumstance would allow me the chance
  Most happily would I accept,

And see your good wife and the lasses and lads
  Who mostly are strangers to me,
But some future day I'll come over that way
  I certainly will when I'm free.

You also must come to see us my old boy,
  I'd bear all the cost if I could,
Your expenses defray and everything pay
  Most readily, gladly I would.

But I, like yourself, have no cash thus to spare,
  I earn what I get at my trade,
I cannot boast wealth, but thank God I have health,
  Although I no fortune have made.

But I must conclude and draw now to a close,
  My letter has grown much too long,
And perhaps you will say " Some parts are too gay
  " And others more sermon than song."

Howe'er that may be my last verse I now write,
  That is for the present you know,
At once then, dear Bill, with a hearty good will
  Farewell.

                    FROM YOUR DEAR BROTHER JOE.

ON DEATH.

Suggested by the early decease of the Rev. J—— S——,
of Reading.   March, 1878.

Death visits all the human race,
In ev'ry age, in ev'ry place,
   His ravages are known ;
In palaces of Kings he treads
And sceptred hands and crowned heads
   Must abdicate the throne.

The affluent, the rich and great,
Must yield alike to stubborn fate,
   With those of humbler name ;
Position, place, nor rank nor power
Can turn aside the dreaded hour,
   It comes on all the same.

The Peasant, Peer and man of thought
By death alike are set at nought,
   Distinctions all are vain :
None can escape his powerful hand
Nor he that rules, nor tills the land,
   Nor he that ploughs the main.

Decrepitude with beauty fall,
And none can disobey the call ;
   The coward and the brave
Are doomed to feel the dreadful sting
Of this all-conq'ring tyrant King,
   His claims he will not waive.

Unmoved by bribes (relentless fate)
He takes no riches from the great,
   But scorns them with disdain :
Elizabeth, Old England's Queen,
Cried out in anguish strong and keen,
   "Oh ! ease me of my pain."

" This moment I will thousands give,
" If I on earth may longer live
    " My evil ways to mend."
But Death regarded not her prayer,
She passed away in dark despair,
    O ! sad and bitter end.

The Soldier on the battle field
Though conq'ring, all to Death must yield
    And lay his weapons by :
In vain the cannon's booming roar,
His reign extends from shore to shore,
    To all beneath the sky.

The Sailor on the rippling wave,
Whose ship the peaceful waters lave,
    Thinks not of danger near :
But suddenly the skies grow dark,
The winds now menace his frail bark
    And fill his heart with fear.

The surging waves in foaming pride,
Now beat against that vessel's side
    And now sweep o'er the deck :
The Sailors, with the ship go down,
And in the gurgling waters drown
    And Death reigns o'er the wreck.

In ev'ry land his victims throng,
With giant strides he tramps along,
    Diseases with him brings :
And desolation marks his path
As o'er the earth in vengeful wrath
    The pestilence he flings.

His potent sway all nations own,
The torrid clime, the frigid zone,
    Wherever life appears
His conquests spread the earth around,
With ruin he doth strew the ground
    And fill the world with tears.

The quiet home, the peaceful cot,
Where calm contentment is the lot
  Of those who dwell within,
Sometimes is broken up by death ;
And sudden is the parting breath
  The penalty of sin.

The lovely child so sweet and fair,
With ruby lips and flowing hair,
  Full cheeks and laughing eyes,
Turns pale within its mother's arms
And losing all its former charms
  Droops, languishes and dies.

The maiden flushed with youthful bloom,
Gives indications of the gloom
  That soon around will spread ;
Her eyes wax dim, her cheeks grow pale,
Her strength declines, her spirits fail,
  And shortly she is dead.

The youth, though now endued with strength,
Becomes disease's prey at length,
  And all his vigour flies :
The Mother watches by her son,
Fearing his race on earth is run,
  And as she fears he dies.

The Father, too, in manhood's prime
(As though existence were a crime)
  Is smitten with disease :
Upon his bed in anguish turns,
As he with raging fever burns,
  And none can give him ease.

He languishes awhile in pain,
Thinks health will soon return again,
  And all his strength restore ;
But hope deludes him : 'tis in vain,
Death terminates his mortal pain
  And friends his loss deplore.

The Wife now mourns her husband dead,
And bitter tears the children shed
  As o'er his grave they bend ;
So quickly torn from their embrace,
They here no more shall see his face,
  What pangs their spirits rend.

Oh ! Death, how wonderful art thou,
How dark thy form, how stern thy brow,
  Thy grasp, how firm and cold ;
At sight of thee poor mortals sink
In deep dismay ; and backward shrink
  The timid and the bold.

O ! could I paint thy visage here,
As thou to me wilt soon appear,
  What colours should I use ?
Shall I meet thee in terror drest,
Or wilt thou smiling bid me rest
  And joys around diffuse ?

To those who live their lives aright,
Thou comest as an Angel bright,
  In purest white arrayed ;
Immortal gladness with thee brings,
Triumphantly the Christian sings,
  He fears no dreadful shade.

Our Minister, who lately died,
And cross'd cold Jordan's swelling tide
  To regions bright and fair,
Felt no foreboding, fearful gloom,
As he approach'd the dismal tomb,
  For Christ was with him there.

The Saviour Whom while here he served,
With strength divine his spirit nerved
  And all his fears allayed ;
Amid affliction's piercing woes,
And 'mid death's agonizing throes
  His mind on God was stayed.

In life he held Religion's cause,
And strove to keep her sacred laws,
  And her commands obey;
In faith and patience kept his soul,
Until he reach'd the final goal
  Of everlasting day.

In life's mid-day his race was run,
The Cross laid by, the glory won,
  Eternal in the skies;
With Saints and Angels there to dwell,
In raptures that no tongue can tell,
  O! lovely paradise.

Though we may mourn his absence here,
He fills in heaven a better sphere,
  In realms of bliss above;
Removed from this distressing life,
Where oft are bickering and strife,
  To where is nought but love.

Of her life-partner now bereft,
The Wife a widow hence is left,
  But God is still her friend;
And though He seem to hide His face,
He will support her with His grace
  And keep her to the end.

His providence may seem severe,
In taking those we hold most dear,
  But 'tis for some wise end;
To make us mindful of His power,
That we may serve Him every hour
  And on His love depend.

To wean our hearts from things below,
That we more lasting joys may know,
  Than those of time and sense;
To make our best affections rise,
T'wards Him Who rules earth, sea and skies
  And soon will call us hence

To stir us up to watch and pray,
That when Death comes (come when he may),
   We, too, may safely die ;
Take off our armour, drop the shield,
Lay by the sword and leave the field,
   For glory in the sky.

O ! may we wisely, one and all,
The lesson learn, obey the call,
   Which now sounds in our ears :
And turn to God without delay,
Serve Him with gladness every day,
   All through this vale of tears.

Then when this transient life is o'er,
And our frail pulses beat no more,
   We'll mount the upper skies :
And there with all the ransomed sing,
While heaven's eternal arches ring,
   As our hosannas rise.

Belovëd Pastor, now farewell,
Till we with thee shall meet and dwell
   Around yon glorious throne ;
A long eternity to spend,
Where happiness can never end,
   And parting is unknown.

May God sustain the Widow here,
Her anguish soothe, her spirits cheer,
   Till earth and time are o'er ;
When free from sorrow, care and pain,
In bliss unbounded she shall reign,
   With him that's gone before.

THE THICK CLOUD.

March 7th, 1889.

PART I.

As if the Sun had quench'd his noontide ray,
   And wrapp'd the world in thickest folds of night,
As if the Moon and Stars had pass'd away
   And all had faded from my wistful sight,
A gloom unbearable came stealing o'er me
When she my Angel-Wife pass'd on before me.

Yes, went before me to that other land,
   "From whese far bourn" 'tis said none e'er returns (?)
And join'd the gentle, loving sister band
   (For kindred souls the human spirit yearns).
The night that led me into deepest mourning
Was nought to her but Heaven's brightest morning.

Though *that* of course was hidden from my sight
   I could not see nor could I *then believe ;*
My joys were blotted out, 'twas darkest night,
   No consolation did my heart relieve,
I nothing then could do but sit repining,
No faintest ray upon my spirit shining.

So sudden and so crushing was the blow,
   So unexpected all that then took place,
Without a moment's warning thus laid low ;
   The bloom of health returning to her face,
The light of joy within her eyes was beaming,
And ne'er more cheerful was her spirit seeming.

To him, her husband, she had said "Good-bye"
   As he to her when leaving for the day—
The farewell kiss, the mutual glancing eye,
   As from the other each must break away ;
She waved her hand and threw her kisses to him,
They were Love's shafts and pierced most kindly through him.

Ah ! little did he know they were the last
   That she to him in love would ever throw,
As backwards smiling he to her did cast
   Affection's token and his own love show ;
No thought, presentiment, or slightest warning
Had he upon that uneventful morning.

Her parting kisses thus she threw to me,
   And watch'd me up the road till out of sight,
We should no more each other's presence see
   Till darkness should succeed the fading light,
Till night o'er all his sable wings be spreading
And stars on earth their feeble rays be shedding.

Thus did we part on that ill-fated day,
   And thus our love towards each other show,
And neither knew what just before us lay,
   That one should fill with bliss, the other woe :
We both were looking forward years before us
Not knowing what was closely hanging o'er us.

O'er her a crown, but o'er myself a cross,
   A cross 'neath which like One of old I sank,
Her blissful gain was my unhappy loss ;
   The cup of sorrow then I deeply drank,
My well-nigh bursting heart with anguish swelling,
Grief all too great beyond the power of telling.

The cheering word, the pleasant parting smile,
   The gentle pressure of the hand in mine,
Revealed a love that did my heart beguile
   When on my path the sun refused to shine ;
When adverse circumstances would oppress me
That loving smile would always seem to bless me.

All through that ne'er-to-be-forgotten day
   In streaming torrents fell the drenching rain,
The angry storm-clouds hover'd o'er my way
   And made me long for home and her again ;
To home my weary heart was ever turning,
Where truest love for my return was yearning.

I knew that there I should most welcome be,
   However others might my presence spurn,
That there at least one heart beat true to me
   And ever waited for my glad return,
When she at once with comforts would surround me,
And though sometimes depressed, glad joy soon found me

There with my children and my faithful wife,
   When ended were the labours of the day,
And all forgotten was the world's wild strife,
   The storms that sometimes round one's self would play,
Within my own four walls in peace reclining,
Light, love, and joy upon my spirit shining.

There she would busily her needle ply
   (No idle moments would she ever know),
Or swiftly would the shooting shuttle fly,
   And just as rapidly the stitches grow ;
Thus would she toil with ever thrifty fingers,
The picture still within my memory lingers.

While round about her would the children play,
   Contentment smiling in their very looks,
The happy evening thus would wear away ;
   Myself be conning o'er my fav'rite books,
Or in my easy chair with pencil rhyming,
While on my knees the children would be climbing.

Ah ! yes, at home, 'twas there I long'd to be
   With her and them that I their joys might share,
My jaded heart at once would feel more free
   And, beating lighter, cast aside its care ;
The little worries that so much perplex one
And seem incessantly to plague and vex one.

I ever there a sweet asylum found
   A quiet refuge from the world's wild din,
There far removed from each discordant sound
   With all on earth most dear to me shut in
My heart found rest ; forgetting all its sadness,
Encircled with an atmosphere of gladness.

As shines the Pole-star out upon the sea,
   Inspiring him who toils upon the wave,
As o'er the bounding, foaming billows he
   (Though storms sometimes may round his vessel rave)
Doth guide her course, assisted by its gleaming,
As through the gloom its rays are gently beaming.

Or as the moon, with cheering silvery light,
   When climbing ardently the Eastern steep,
Drives back the baneful shadows of the night,
   Which now a more respectful distance keep,
As overhead in queenly splendour riding,
Or 'neath dark clouds serenely she is gliding.

Thus shone my home to me when far away,
   Or toiling wearily along the road
When moon nor stars would cast a single ray ;
   My horse he struggling with a heavy load,
The wheels sunk in the mud and stiffly grinding,
As we our homeward way were slowly winding.

As o'er the desert's sandy, vast expanse,
   When smitten by the sun's most scorching heat,
The trav'ller casts his eye and sees by chance
   A place of refuge and a kind retreat
Of shady palm trees in the distance bending,
To his glad sight their sweet enchantment lending.

So to my weary heart would home appear,
   An oasis upon life's desert plain,
Where I could rest and my sad spirits cheer,
   Restored to her and her sweet love again ;
There peace o'er all her snowy wings extending,
From early morning to the sun's descending.

Such was my home to me ; and on that day
   When last I broke from her most kind embrace
And did to her my last addresses pay,
   Imprinting my last kisses on her face ;
Her face, which then was warm, responsive, living,
And gave to me what I to her was giving.

I

Yes, on that dreary day, shone brighter far
  Across my cheerless, dull, and gloomy way,
Than finest radiance of the moon or star :
  I yearned intensely for my home that day,
Which in the morning I had left so cheerful,
And nought occurred to make my spirit fearful.

I felt like one who out upon the sea,
  Returning from a far and distant shore,
Desires his own dear native land to see
  And meet his friends and kindred there once more,
Who as its rock-bound coast is hourly nearing,
Beholds with joy its tall white cliffs appearing.

Or him who out upon the burning plain,
  Without a shelter from the sultry rays
As he with aching feet toils on again ;
  When lo ! there meets his now enraptured gaze
A grove of palm trees in the distance swaying,
The refuge there for which he had been praying.

Thus did my fancy picture my abode
  When toiling in the darkness and the rain,
In winter time belated on the road,
  Desire sometimes amounting e'en to pain !
To reach my home, with comforts there surrounded,
This was the vision that my thoughts then bounded.

As points the needle to the distant pole,
  And ever turns its trembling shaft that way,
Some strange mysterious influence doth control
  Its hidden properties both night and day ;
In light or dark, awake or soundly sleeping,
That needle point is always Northwards keeping.

And homewards thus my heart would ever turn,
  Controll'd by forces hidden and unseen,
Magnetic forces that would make me yearn
  For home and her, though miles were us between ;
When far away their power was ever present
Directing homewards, which was always pleasant.

Yes, always pleasant, though I might be sad,
  Things sometimes would conspire to make me so,
To think of home and her would make me glad
  And bring me consolation in my woe ;
A bow of promise to my spirit given
Like that which spans the stormy vault of heaven.

Or like a glimpse of most delightful blue
  When part the clouds disclosing depths of space,
Where planets, stars, erratic comets, too,
  Run their unending everlasting race
Through fathomless abyss for ever sweeping,
And all unfailing perfect order keeping.

Or like the light that through the opening breaks
  And falls upon the gladsome earth below,
Creation sleeping all at once awakes
  And everywhere sweet tints of colour show ;
A gleam of sunshine o'er the landscape stealing,
Its hidden beauties all at once revealing.

The star, the moon, the palm trees' pleasant shade,
  The spot of blue, the sweet descending light,
Which all around such transformation made ;
  Such home was ever to my grateful sight
" A thing of beauty and a joy for ever,"
Made by God's blessing and my own endeavour.

Such were my feelings on that tearful night,
  When she my best belovëd passed away,
To those fair regions of unclouded light,
  To that bright home of everlasting day,
With Saints and Angels there for ever dwelling,
Whose joys surpass imagination's telling.

I left the town depressed and much cast down,
  The weather all that day had been so bad,
And circumstances seem'd so much to frown,
  All things conspired to make one dull and sad :
The clouds' dark aspect and incessant raining
One's sense of comfort would be ever paining.

I 2

One thought alone upon that wild March day,
   Like sunshine on my lonely spirit fell,
And cast within its heart inspiring ray
   That yonder in my home all things were well,
That there shone light and love and joy and gladness
Which soon would dissipate my gloom and sadness.

I hasten'd on, impelled by strong desire,
   Most anxious on that night my home to reach,
In comfort there before the blazing fire,
   And list'ning to my dear's most welcome speech,
Who to my woes with sympathetic pleasure
Would then give heed, and comfort without measure.

The daylight passed, and now arose the night,
   Dark threat'ning clouds still hanging in the sky,
Nor moon, nor stars, did offer once their light,
   The wind like madden'd furies rushing by;
Like them as in despair most loudly raving
And in a manner most uncouth behaving.

It howl'd the shudd'ring frighten'd trees among,
   It shrieked and whistled in the startled air,
Unearthly wild the wailing tones that rung
   The hollow accents of a deep despair;
Anon and more subdued 'twas feebly groaning
And in low undertones was faintly moaning.

O! how I long'd to reach my distant home,
   That kindly shelter from the storm's rude blast,
The driving rain, the wind that still would come,
   The low'ring sky with inky clouds o'ercast;
The angry elements around me raging
And all my feeble powers at once engaging.

PART II.

While thus without the evening passed with me,
  Within at home the cheerful firelight glow'd,
My wife and children snugly taking tea,
  Talking of him who absent on the road.
All anxious for my welcome glad returning
As I for home most ardently was yearning.

All through that day most cheerful had she been,
  At times quite sportive with her little maids,
In her own home she was the happy queen,
  She ruled the lights, was mistress of the shades :
Her presence brought the sunshine to the dwelling
Her absence those bright beams at once dispelling.

Ah ! yes, she with her little daughters play'd,
  And entertained them with her harmless fun
And for them each she also dolls' clothes made ;
  She loved them both and equally each one,
No partial spirit would she ever show them
But both alike and equal ever know them.

Each meal enjoyed, but most of all her tea,
  Tea ever was with her a fav'rite meal,
The crock'ry's jingle would sweet music be
  Like gladsome wedding bells' delightful peal,
Whose clear wild melody with tones sonorous
In rich vibrations breaking grandly o'er us.

How often have I heard her fondly say,
  When list'ning to the rattle of the spoons,
As all arranging on the shining tray
  (Herself most neat and trim) on afternoons
" I love to hear the tea things merry jingle
" Their welcome sounds with my glad feelings mingle."

The kettle singing on the polished grate ;
  The cheerful lamp ; the firelight's ruddy glow ;
The butter'd toast upon the fender plate
  That did such appetizing fragrance throw,
Which with the tea's delightful odour blending
Through one's whole being would be comfort sending.

The picture needed but one other touch,
　To give it finish and complete the scene,
It was that he whom they desired so much
　Could with them on that afternoon have been,
The family circle then had been completed
And all in comfort round the table seated.

But he though absent was in spirit there,
　And occupied his own accustomed place,
All unperceived, unnoticed in his chair,
　His form concealed and hidden was his face;
Yet there he seemed to be with them uniting,
With them rejoicing and with them delighting.

It seemed as though on that eventful day
　Two spirits I possessed; the one was glad
With those at home; the other far away,
　With obstacles beset and feeling sad;
The one with loved ones, wife and children, near him,
The other far removed, no ray to cheer him.

So strong at times imagination grows,
　And seems to take us where we fain would be,
That by its aid the heart forgets its woes,
　The bounding spirit feels more light and free;
Its wondrous power the being seems to sever,
Dividing that which should be parted never.

But though its strength is thus so very great,
　It is but brief and cannot long endure,
And recollection leads us back to fate,
　Unites us with our former self once more;
'Tis then we see 'twas but the mind's illusion,
And we the victims of a vain delusion.

Thus was it with myself that stormy night,
　I yearned until I fancied I was there,
The happy children and herself in sight,
　My heart forgetting for the while its care;
But soon in darkness ended the sweet vision,
The wind still howling round as in derision.

But there sat they, herself and little girls,
   In comfort round the table taking tea,
Dear Aggie's rosy face and Hetty's curls ;
   A pale good natured loving face had she
The Mother ; on her children ever doting
And in their int'rests all her powers devoting.

And now as ended was that ev'ning meal,
   The things were cleansed and turn'd upon the tray,
Then all were wiped, cups, saucers, spoons and steel,
   Each in its place then neatly put away ;
The table-cloth was brushed or gently shaken,
Placed on the shelf from whence it had been taken.

And there they were, the children full of glee,
   She sporting with them, sharing in their fun,
The happy moments passed most pleasantly,
   The day seemed ending as the day begun ;
No sign, no warning, and no slightest token
That life's frail thread that ev'ning would be broken.

And now she fancied she could hear the sound
   Of rumbling wheels upon the gravel stones,
At once their spirits would yet lighter bound
   And quite ecstatic were the children's tones,
With rapture their young eyes would shine and glisten
As she addressed them with " My dears, hark ! listen,

" What is that I can hear, what can it be,
   " I think it must be Dadda drawing near
" And very soon his presence we shall see,
   " He with us shortly will again appear ;
" It must be he, the sound is drawing nearer,
" 'Tis more distinct, 'tis louder and 'tis clearer."

That instant, sudden as the lurid glare,
   That flashes from the storm cloud in the sky,
When rising vapours fill the stagnant air,
   No moving wind, no stirring breezes nigh,
She backwards fell, without a moment's warning,
As none had I when leaving in the morning.

How near is Heaven to the rolling earth?
    Maybe it stretches through the realms of space
Encircling all that are of mortal birth,
    Encompassing entire the human race;
The unseen world may be around and near us,
Like the pure light to gladden and to cheer us.

And how uncertain is our fleeting breath,
    How thin the veil which hides that world from this,
But one step only 'tween ourselves and death,
    'Tis but a curtain screens that state of bliss:
And sometimes O! how sudden the transition
From mortal life to beatific vision.

O! not my wheels was that which then she heard,
    But Angel pinions sounding in her ear,
Love's messengers had come to bring her word
    That she in Paradise must then appear;
Love's King had sent them; they in love obeying,
Love's willing wings the summons glad conveying.

Ah! yes, it was their wings she heard that night,
    Love's chariot wheels that sounded in her ear
And filled her spirit with a strange delight,
    Just when she thought my van was drawing near:
'Twas then the Angels with glad rapture flying
Took her sweet spirit without pain of dying.

All unobserved those shining Angels came
    From their bright home to take her spirit thence;
Those silent messengers of living flame
    Concealed themselves from every mortal sense,
To her alone the gladsome message bringing,
Her ears alone with heavenly music ringing.

Yes, none but her the heavenly sounds could hear,
    And none but her the Angel forms could see,
None else suspecting e'en that they were near;
    No other sight or sound they thought could be
Than what was patent to the carnel senses
And all this mortal life surrounds and fences.

"Twas she alone that heard their rustling wings,
  Within her soul the rapturous music broke,
As they the message from the King of Kings
  In gentle tones to her glad spirit spoke ;
They whispered to her as their forms bent o'er her,
Then to the skies on love's soft wings they bore her.

They bore her to the realms of cloudless day,
  The rest remaining to God's people there,
With Him and them for evermore to stay
  And all their happiness henceforth to share :
O ! bliss supreme ! O ! joy beyond the telling,
In that fair home for ever to be dwelling.

For ever there 'mid scenes surpassing thought,
  With all the ransomed and the Angel throng.
Her happy spirit they that evening sought,
  They took her to the land of light and song :
All unexpectedly the news was brought her,
But *she was ready* and away they caught her.

They caught her hence from weakness and from pain,
  From sorrow's night, from loneliness and gloom,
They caught her thence, beyond life's stormy main
  To fields of light and everlasting bloom,
That land of beauty and of bliss supernal,
That home of joy whose pleasures are eternal.

Dear, quiet soul, for ever now at rest,
  Sweet gentle heart, at home in comfort there,
With kindred spirits thou art ever blest,
  Released for ever from life's carking care ;
No unkind circumstance shall there oppress thee,
Nor disappointment ever more distress thee.

There thou art safe and there we leave thee now,
  Still looking forward to the time when we
With fadeless diadems upon our brow,
  Restored for ever to thy love and thee
Shall meet again 'mid Heaven's eternal splendour,
Roam its glad fields and ceaseless praises render.

With thee for ever then we shall unite,
 There in that home of beauty and of joy,
Beyond the reach of sorrow, pain and night
 'Mid purest pleasures that can never cloy ;
Raptures beyond the finite mind's conceiving,
Past fancy's range and e'en the heart's believing.

———

PART III.

But O ! the gloom that settled down on me
 As I drew near my home that dreadful night
And there the Doctor's carriage lights could see,
 Throwing their baleful lustre on my sight
Like two large angry eyes with fury gleaming
Upon myself most ominously beaming.

There in the roadway, just outside my gate,
 His carriage stood ; the lights' portentous glare
Burst on my vision like a flash of fate,
 And filled my spirit with a blank despair,
O ! what is wrong, what now can be transpiring?
Alas ! alas ! my darling was expiring.

O ! what a rush of thoughts within my mind
 (As yet I knew not what had taken place),
I seemed impressed that fate had been unkind ;
 The door was closed and hid her pale sweet face,
I nothing knew and only could be guessing,
Held in suspense, my thoughts were most distressing.

She came not to the door to let me in,
 As was her custom when I reach'd my home,
With kindly welcome which my heart would win
 (She always was most glad to see me come).
" Well, dear, I'm glad to see you home returning,
" You must be tired and for your supper yearning."

Within that silent room sat she my wife,
    Her form reclining on the sofa there,
A contest had been fought 'tween death and life,
    He was the victor, she his victim fair ;
One single shaft from his most fatal quiver
Had pierced her brain, and closed her eyes for ever.

I stood without, still kept in dark suspense,
    None seemed to know that her sweet life was gone
Beyond the reach of every mortal sense
    To other blessëd and more blissful dawn ;
No sight nor sound of her my senses greeting,
One question only my sad thoughts repeating.

At length the Doctor came from out the room,
    My unwashed hand in his he kindly took,
A tone of sympathy he did assume ;
    He gave a most compassionating look,
Asked for a chair in which I might be seated,
As I of him some kind relief entreated.

" I fear to tell you " then he kindly said,
    " What in your absence has this day transpired,
" Your wife's no more, she's numbered with the dead,
    " Ere I could reach your home she had expired ;
" But had she not I could no more assist her
" Than what was done by her devoted sister."

I rush'd into the room from whence he came,
    I scarcely knew what I was doing then,
I spoke to her, I called her by her name,
    I stroked her hair, I spoke to her again ;
It seem'd to me as though she was but sleeping
And all her senses still in her own keeping.

She still was sitting on the sofa there,
    Her head reclining as in peaceful sleep,
The sofa she preferr'd before a chair
    And to that sofa she would ever keep ;
" That dear old sofa," she would oft be saying,
" Is *such* a comfort."   On it she was staying.

I knelt beside her feeling lone and sad,
   I took her soft warm hand within my own
(It still was warm although no life it had)
   The hand that to me had such kindness shown :
I pressed it to my lips and kissed it often,
The more I kissed the more 'twould seem to soften.

I kissed her forehead and I kissed her face,
   Her forehead bright as polish'd marble shone,
Her slender form I also did embrace
   And still I called her " Darling, dear, my own ; "
I could not think her dead, but only dreaming,
She soon would wake and quite herself be seeming.

The time wore on, the evening passed away,
   She did not wake as I had hoped she would.
She still outstretched in quiet stillness lay,
   Myself the while in most distressful mood ;
And still as on the weary hours would lengthen
My fears yet stronger grew and still would strengthen.

We bore her gently to a room upstairs,
   Where she might rest in peace and undisturbed,
Untroubled by our sorrows and our cares,
   All unmolested and all imperturbed ;
A quiet chamber where she still might slumber,
While I all-wakeful night's long hours might number.

O ! night of nights, most dreadful night to me,
   No night like that had I ere known before,
Such night again O ! may I never see,
   From such may I be kept for evermore ;
Till nights of gloom and darkness are all ended
And with Eternity old Time has blended.

All through that ne'er-to-be-forgotten night
   (As through that ne'er-to-be-forgotten day)
The tempest raged ; the wind with mad affright
   Howl'd round the house where I distracted lay ;
It shook the windows and the doors it rattled
As if the elements together battled.

Anon, a lull, and then as in mad freak,
   The pause was follow'd by a dreadful roar ;
And this again by most unearthly shriek,
   That whistled through the keyhole in the door.
And now in hollow tones most dismal moaning
Within the chimney like some monster groaning.

And then again 'twould seem to sob and sigh,
   And oft I started wildly in my bed,
I thought I heard my poor dear Darling cry ;
   So humanlike the sounds that overhead,
Around, below, inside and out the dwelling,
The awful secrets of the night were telling.

My two dear little maids who saw her die
   (Although they knew not what had taken place),
Both slept within the same room as did I ;
   They were mere babes, not long begun life's race,
The elder in a bed made up beside us
The younger lay in ours and did divide us.

All through that night dear Aggie soundly slept,
   But Hetty sometimes woke and she would cry,
And although long and piteously she wept
   She never once enquired the reason why
Her Mamma was not there and still beside her
Her griefs to soothe whatever might betide her.

Her silence pained me, as I fear'd she knew
   Her Mother now was past the reach of call,
Had past from sight and out of hearing too
   Beyond her children and beyond us all ;
Beyond this life with all its faults and failings,
Its bitter griefs, its sorrows and heart wailings.

Ah ! yes, poor little dear, she must have known,
   That she, her best of friends, had passed away ;
The night before, when we were there alone,
   It seems she woke and listen'd as she lay
To what her Auntie and myself were saying
Of her who lifeless in the house was staying.

We thought her sleeping till we heard her cry.
  The cry betoken'd much distress and grief.
She knew her Mother was no longer nigh
  To soothe her sorrows and to give relief,
To ease her pain or comfort her when crying
As when beside her she all night was lying.

At length that dismal dreary night was past,
  And once again the growing light of day
Its cheering radiance in my chamber cast,
  Driving night's shadows and night's gloom away,
Restoring life and beauty to creation
Where all night long seem'd nought but desolation.

But O ! how painful when dear Aggie woke
  All unaware of what had taken place,
As rising in her bed to me she spoke,
  Sweet childish innocence upon her face ;
Fresh as the light that in the room was streaming
Her happy countenance with joy was beaming.

"Good morning, Dadda," smilingly she said,
  "Good morning, darling," I to her replied,
She thought, of course, her Mamma was in bed
  As heretofore and sleeping by her side ;
She nothing knew of all the pain and sorrow
That must befall her on that dreadful morrow.

She did not know the precious life had fled,
  Though she was present when her Mother died,
Witness'd the shudder and the drooping head,
  The hands first clenched then hanging by her side ;
'Twas thought she had but fainted ; this was told her,
She'd soon be well and they again behold her.

She turn'd towards her Mother's vacant place,
  And saw with great surprise she was not there,
How changed at once was that dear little face
  As she enquired "Where is my Mamma, where?
"Is she better, and is she down stairs sleeping,
"There by herself all through the dark night keeping?"

My heart was full, I scarce could make reply,
   At length I said "She is no better dear,"
The light of joy then faded from her eye
   And in its place there glisten'd now a tear ;
The poor child seem'd to know, my manner told her
That she was gone ; she should no more behold her.

Poor little dears, I never can forget,
   The anguish then I felt on their account
As on my own ; the sorrow and regret
   That she was gone, on love's soft wings to mount
The blissful skies ; her mantle on us falling,
Her absence paining, but her spirit calling.

I can't forget nor can I e'er express,
   How then I felt towards the little dears ;
I pray'd that He Who gave and took would bless
   And guide them safely through this vale of tears,
Till they in Heaven their long-lost Mother meeting
'Mid joys ineffable each other greeting.

They saw how poignant was their Father's grief,
   How bitter and deep-seated his distress,
They scann'd his face for traces of relief
   (The truth, of course, they could as yet but guess),
Their bitter grief was by my own augmented
And mine by theirs till I was half demented.

O ! how I dreaded that I must make known
   The dismal tidings to the little dears,
That she was gone and we were left alone
   Without her presence in the coming years ;
Without her love, her sympathy and gladness
Our griefs to soothe and dissipate our sadness.

Without her counsel when we were perplex'd,
   Without her kindness when our hearts were sad,
Without her patience when we might be vex'd,
   Without her cheerfulness to make us glad,
Without her wisdom and her kind endeavour
Without her virtues and her all for ever.

Ne'er did a woman love her children more
  Than she did them, those two dear little things,
And never did two children e'er before
  More ardent love return; sweet love that brings
True happiness within the heart and dwelling
All other joys outweighing and excelling.

The breakfast clear'd I took them by the hand
  (Each little hand I took within my own),
I talk'd to them about the " Better Land,"
  Where holy Angels and the good alone
For ever dwell amid glad scenes supernal
Whose light ne'er fades all beauteous and vernal.

I told them then upon that woful day,
  That she had pass'd to that bright home of love,
And that her poor dear lifeless body lay
  In quiet stillness in the room above;
The body left, the living soul translated
To yonder skies where loved ones for her waited.

And then I led them to that quiet room
  (Each little hand still held within my own),
The blinds were drawn which but increased the gloom
  And still the winds would sob and sigh and moan,
All things against us then conspired together;
Gloom reigned within, without the angry weather.

I led them on and to each little maid
  Spoke words of comfort their sad hearts to cheer,
" She's still and cold, but do not be afraid,
  " She loves you still and so you need not fear;
" Her face is pale, but still a beauty lingers
" Untouch'd as yet by Death's cold icy fingers."

The room we enter'd where she sleeping lay,
  Poor little dears what must they then have felt?
My own sad feelings on that dreadful day
  Were such that all my manhood seem'd to melt
To tears of grief, to sorrow and to sighing,
That she in Death's relentless grasp was lying.

I kiss'd her dear, kind, cold and rigid face,
    'Twas now but clay, the spirit having fled
To its own native and appointed place,
    With all the dear deceased whom we call dead,
But who in fact were never so much living
As they are now ; glad songs of praises giving.

And then the children did as I had done,
    Their little eyes abrim with scalding tears,
Which now o'erflow and down the crystals run ;
    'Twas most distressing they so young in years,
So young to bear such pangs as they were feeling
Their grief so great seem'd past the power of healing.

O ! could that gentle spirit have returned
    And seen those two dear children standing there,
How would she in her heart of hearts have yearned
    With pity, love and kind maternal care,
Towards them as they both stood by her weeping
Their eyes upon her rigid features keeping.

PART IV.

How strong the sympathy of human souls
    Towards each other none can ever tell,
Wave upon wave of deepest feeling rolls
    O'er the spirit, when in the flesh we dwell ;
But how 'twill be when from the flesh we sever
We know not ; but *believe* 'twill last for ever.

Nor do we know if loved ones e'er return
    In any way that sympathy to show,
With those their friends whom they have left to yearn
    For something better than this life below ;
But we *believe* that often they are near us
Soul acting upon soul and thus they cheer us.

K

And might not she that morning have been there
 (A special favour by her Lord bestow'd)
To soothe her children and relieve their care,
 In some way lighten sorrow's heavy load ;
In some kind way their sad young hearts sustaining
And still to them her purest love retaining ?

We do not know so close the veil is drawn,
 When sever'd is life's last connecting link,
We feel as though they had for ever gone
 In dark oblivion's dismal depths to sink ;
So keen our anguish and so great our sorrow,
'Tis dark to-day and darker still to-morrow.

Thy way O ! God, is in the mighty sea,
 Thy path is in the vast and trackless deep,
Thy footsteps there are lost ; we cannot see
 Where Thou dost go, the course that Thou dost keep :
Darkness and clouds are often round about Thee,
Our faith is weak and hence we often doubt Thee.

We doubt Thy goodness when we should believe,
 Thy wisdom question when we should confide,
Impatiently we often pine and grieve,
 Whereas, could we but see the other side
Of that which brings us so much pain and sadness
We often should rejoice for very gladness.

But as time rolls, the light begins to break,
 And hope again lifts up her fallen crest,
Creation's harmonics once more awake,
 Again we feel we are divinely blest ;
Time heals our wounds and drives away our sorrows
Hope from the future sweet enchantment borrows.

And faith and confidence once more return,
 Our joys come back and life grows bright again,
Heaven's purposes at last we now discern ;
 In all our anguish and our grief and pain
He sought our good ; He nothing meant but kindness,
This then was hidden through our own purblindness.

To earth and earthly things we are so prone,
　So taken up with what this life can give,
That were we left but to ourselves alone
　No true incentive prompting us to live ;
We soon might then forget our destination
Our noble calling and our high vocation.

But trouble comes (an Angel in disguise)
　And sad bereavements sometimes on us fall,
Our dearest friends are caught up to the skies,
　To us they beckon and to us they call :
Life's fascinating spells and vain delusions
Then lose their hold, and vanish Time's illusions.

Love thus presides at our life's guiding helm,
　And steers us safely 'mid its sunken reefs,
And though sometimes our sorrows us o'erwhelm,
　Our hearts quite sinking 'neath our woes and griefs ;
Yet *afterwards* when fuller light is breaking
All for our good we see was wisely making.

But is she gone ?　Will she come back no more ?
　Shall we not see her in the house again ?
To cheer us with her presence as before
　As queen in her own happy home to reign ;
Our lives to brighten and our hearts to gladden
When things distress us and conspire to sadden ?

Ah ! yes, she's gone and never can return,
　In fleshly form or corporeal frame,
However much our stricken hearts may yearn
　She will not come as heretofore she came ;
With sense of touch and tangible appealing
To our discernment thus herself revealing.

We know full well she never can come thus,
　Her body in the quiet churchyard lies,
No power has *that* again to visit us
　With smiling countenance and beaming eyes ;
No will, no sentiment and no affection
'Tis but dead matter and all imperfection.

K 2

But who can tell but that her spirit may
  (Her own true self immortal and divine)
Hover at times about our lonely way
  With gracious purpose and intent benign ;
Her kind assistance in some way to lend us
With love's devotion as of old attend us ?

Sometimes it seems as though she still was here,
  As in the days gone by she used to be,
Her voice at times we fancy we can hear
  And e'en her presence sometimes think we see ;
Sometimes she seems to come and sit beside us,
Bursting the barriers that by death divide us.

Ere since the night she closed her eyes in death,
  And slept the sleep from which none ever wake,
And yielded up life's transient, fleeting breath,
  As bubbles rise and on the waters break ;
They to the surface from the depths ascending
Seek their own element and with it blending.

Yes, since we were of her dear form bereft,
  I seem at times to feel her presence more ;
Though she this earthly, mortal life has left,
  Somehow she seems more present than before ;
Upstairs and down, inside and out the dwelling
Still there she seems a mystery past my telling.

Sometimes I fancy I can see her face,
  Radient with smiles still looking into mine,
As there she sits in her accustomed place,
  Just as of old ; so gracious and benign
The old affection in her eyes still beaming.
O ! is it real, or am I only dreaming?

Her mystic presence seems in every room,
  And oftentimes my heart is half afraid,
But only so when night's descending gloom
  Fills all the house with dark nocturnal shade ;
'Tis then a sense of dread upon me creeping,
Fills me with terror and prevents me sleeping.

Though why we should be fearful I scarce know,
   She would not hurt us if she had the power,
But rather would her loving kindness show,
   And seek to cheer us in life's dullest hour ;
She would do nothing that could e'er alarm us,
Still less do aught to injure or to harm us.

It must be that the nerves are weak and low,
   That thus we dread the absence of the light,
And such alarm and perturbation show,
   When round us the black curtains of the night
Are drawn by unseen Hand with kind intention,
Nature's arrangement for the mind's suspension.

She would not harm us, why then should we fear ?
   Why should we dread that which would do us good,
If she were plainly to our eyes appear
   (Had she the power I feel quite sure she would)
We could not surely but be much delighted
That her sweet presence we again had sighted.

We then should *know* what now we but *believe*,
   That still she lives in other fairer clime ;
'Twould also much the heart's keen pangs relieve.
   Could we but look beyond the bounds of time
And see her in that home of light and beauty :
Grief then were sin ; thanksgiving be a duty.

Then come sweet spirit to thy earthly home,
   Come back, come often, and stay with us long,
Be with us too when we abroad may roam,
   Restrain us ever when we would go wrong ;
Be with us still as in the days departed,
Kind, sympathetic, and most tenderhearted.

" O ! for the touch of that long vanish'd hand,
   " O ! for the sound of that dear voice now still,"
O ! that her presence fron that other land,
   Our hearts with gladness once again might fill ;
O ! might she come with us once more uniting,
Her joys imparting and our souls delighting.

If thus she came we could not but rejoice ;
   We should not be afraid, no terror feel :
And if 'tis left to her own happy choice
   In some such way she will herself reveal ;
She will not come to trouble or distress us,
Whene'er she comes 'twill be that she may bless us.

But will she come?   She may ; we cannot tell,
   We oft have heard that they come back to earth,
Once more to mingle with their friends that dwell
   Still round the old and dear familiar hearth ;
Where they themselves once had their home and dwelling,
That there they come love's secrets to be telling.

But wherefore should our friends come back to earth,
   What is their mission if they do return?
Is it to make us sad or kindle mirth,
   Give pain, or pleasure? We the truth would learn :
Is it to tell us that they still are living
Proof palpable and clear unto us giving ?

Is it to warn us of some danger near,
   Which we ourselves do not suspect or see,
But which to them is ocular and clear ?
   What we see not to them most clear may be :
They occupy than us a higher standing,
More lofty plane, more elevated landing.

Or is it some impending stroke of fate
   They would from us divert and turn aside,
That thus they do about our pathway wait ?
   Their vision's range must now be vast and wide :
More they must know than when they were but mortal,
More light they have since passing Death's dark portal.

Or maybe 'tis to soothe the widow'd heart,
   And wipe away the little orphan's tear,
Still anxious they to do their loving part
   As when they were in fleshly presence here ;
As when they could be seen and heard about us,
'Twould seem as though they scarce can do without us ;

Nor can they, love's strong ties do still them bind
  Indissolubly to their friends below,
They could not, therefore, but to us be kind
  And still to us love's old devotion show;
Though envious Death our bodies here may sever,
Sweet friendship still endures, unbroken ever.

They may, perhaps, in some most wondrous way,
  Upon our minds their own sweet thoughts impress,
Thoughts quite in keeping with the cheerful day
  And their own blissful, happy state no less;
Thoughts pure and bracing as the morning breezes
When Nature charms and ev'ry object pleases.

How often has the mind been carried hence,
  As by some power we could not understand,
A power outside the realm of mortal sense
  That seems to lift us to some other land;
Or rather state of calm and happy being,
From flesh and sense awhile the spirit freeing.

Sometimes when overborne by grief and care,
  And on our path there falls no ray of light,
When sinks the heart beneath a blank despair
  And all life's joys have faded from our sight;
When night her raven pinions stretching o'er us
Enshrouds with gloom the way that lies before us.

While thus deprest sometimes there breaks around
  " A light that never was on land or sea,"
The spirit rises with exultant bound
  Enfranchised thus and made divinely free;
On faith's strong pinions, Eagle wings outsoaring,
Mounts to the skies with raptured hosts adoring.

As if the sun at midnight hour should rise,
  And fling its glories o'er the sleeping earth,
Waking old Nature with a strange surprise
  At day's nocturnal and untimely birth;
Thus from the mind the shadows all are driven
And Faith looks up and sees her promised Heaven.

But what the cause, whence comes the sudden light,
  That floods the soul with sweet unearthly joy,
Just when immersed in thickest shades of night
  That Hope's existence threaten'd to destroy ;
When Faith was weak and Prayer seem'd unavailing
And doubts and fears against us were prevailing ?

We do not know, although we half divine,
  Since holy writ most plainly doth declare,
That kindred spirits with intent benign
  Do round us throng with ever watchful care ;
Unto the heirs of Promise and Salvation
They minister, with loving emulation.

And may they not in some strange hidden way,
  The human mind be able to control,
Or give us glimpses of some fuller day
  To light at intervals the darken'd soul ;
Our spirits cheering when life's joys are waning
And at all times the burden'd heart sustaining.

And might not thus some unseen spirit friend,
  Whose presence we had lost and mourn'd so long,
In some wise way we cannot comprehend
  Be near us still and still to us belong ;
A foretaste of its own sweet joys imparting,
Just when our own were fading and departing ?

Or maybe 'twas an Angel pure and strong,
  That shook its pinions on us as it past,
Shedding a fragrance that did linger long
  And sweet ; we hoped that it would ever last ;
As from the skies on wings of light descending,
Aflame with love, its earthward course was bending.

They oft are sent from yon' bright courts above,
  On kindest errands to the world below,
With messages of mercy and of love
  And round us they their kind protection throw ;
When all the world against us seems combining
And we lose heart and fall to sad repining.

As when Elijah, wearied with the strife,
   And sick at heart did lay him down to die,
Requesting that the Lord would take his life
   " No better than my fathers were am I " ;
The lion's courage did that day forsake him
And craven fear did quite a coward make him.

And then he fell asleep and soundly slept,
   The forest leaves did serve him for a bed,
And from his face the Sun's hot rays were kept
   By graceful branches bending overhead ;
Beneath a Juniper he thus lay sleeping,
An Angel standing by strict guard was keeping.

And then at length there came a gentle touch,
   At which he woke and wond'ring look'd around
And saw no doubt what did surprise him much ;
   A fire was kindled near him on the ground,
On which by love prepared a cake was baken
And water near that he his thirst might slaken.

He ate and drank and laid him down again,
   The Angel standing by to guard him still,
While he in sleep refresh'd his weary brain ;
   Protected thus he slumber'd on until
With gentle touch again the Angel woke him
And in soft tones of kindest counsel spoke him.

" Arise and eat, the journey is too great,
   " That thou hast taken from the haunts of men,
" Fear not thy enemy's malicious hate,
   " Arise and eat and be thyself again ; "
The Prophet rose, ate, drank and then departed,
Strong as before ; again the lion-hearted.

O ! kind attention by the Angels shown,
   To man when sunk in deepest depths of woe,
When crush'd and prostrate, feeling sad and lone,
   Most timely help and sympathy they show ;
Still as of old mankind they may be blessing
When grief and anguish on our hearts are pressing.

And if the angels, why not saints as well,
   Our old companions in the flesh below,
Who, though they do with us no longer dwell,
   May somehow still their old attachment show ;
They still may cherish feelings kind and tender
And still may wish their services to render.

If man's immortal, then our friends still live,
   And if they live they may possess the power
To visit us and consolation give
   In sorrow's night and trouble's darkest hour ;
Although we see them not they may be near us
To soothe our pangs, to comfort and to cheer us.

Ah ! yes, they may, Love's Master is their king,
   And wondrous powers on them He may bestow ;
To us they oft may life and healing bring
   When we are sinking in the depths of woe ;
They may be able wondrously to aid us,
Since most indulgent is the God Who made us.

Yes, most indulgent for He knows our frame,
   Remembers we are children of the dust
From whence alone our mortal parts first came :
   He is to us both merciful and just ;
He is our God and King, but what we rather
He also is our ever loving *Father*.

Life's possibilities we do not know,
   A mystery enshrouds all things that are
In heaven above and on the earth below,
   The nearest object and most distant star.
The air we breathe, the water we are drinking
Are full of life ; cause for profoundest thinking.

There are more wondrous things in heaven and earth
   Than e'er are dreamt of by the sons of men :
Life lives in all and evermore has birth,
   Life, teeming life, beyond our feeble ken,
Their forms so small defy unaided vision,
And hold our coarser senses in derision.

But there they are, the glass most clearly shows,
  The microscope reveals them to the sight ;
And in like manner may there not be those
  Whose presence would afford us much delight,
Although too fine for sensual perception,
Still near, nor doubt admitting nor deception ?

Lord open Thou our eyes that we may see
  The hidden beauties of the life we live,
May faith a microscope unto us be
  And keener vision to our spirits give,
That we may pierce the gloom that doth enshroud us,
The mists of sense that evermore becloud us.

That if 'tis possible we may behold
  Once more the friends that left us long ago,
That we may see what oft we have been told—
  Departed spirits passing to and fro—
As Jacob saw the angel host ascending
From earth to heaven, from heaven to earth descending.

Or that young man who saw with great dismay
  The Syrian host that gather'd round the place
Where he, Elisha, Israel's Prophet, lay
  In sleep's all-soothing, comforting embrace ;
A hostile army in the night came stealing,
The morning light their presence now revealing.

" Alas ! my Master," then the youth exclaimed,
  " Alas ! my Master, how now shall we do ? "
The surging host with warlike fury flamed,
  And more impatient and determined grew ;
A present to their king the wish'd to make him,
And back to their own country pris'ner take him.

All impurturbed the grand old Prophet rose,
  And unconcern'd look'd out upon the scene ;
Without dismay beheld unnumber'd foes,
  As sharks sometimes are round a vessel seen
When on the craft perchance they know is lying
A person dead, or may be someone dying.

Above that armèd host the Prophet saw
    Another army flaming in the skies,
Which filled his soul with reverential awe ;
    Well might he Syria's puny ranks despise,
Thronging around in atmospheric regions,
Horses and chariots and angelic legions.

This wondrous sight his servant could not see.
    He only saw the Syrian warriors there,
And much alarmed and terrified was he ;
    "Alas ! my Master, how now shall we fare ?"
He nothing saw but fate and evil omen,
Surrounded thus by stern, relentless foemen.

Elisha pray'd, "Lord, open Thou his eyes
    "That he may see, to his glad sight display'd,
"The counter demonstration in the skies,
    "And be no longer fearful or dismayed ;
"That he may see celestial horsemen striding
"Their fiery steeds, and through the heavens riding."

While thus he pray'd the veil was drawn aside,
    Or his course sight to purer vision changed,
And he, too, saw with rapture and with pride
    Those bright battalions in the heavens ranged.
By far outshining Syria's pomp and glory,
As all may know who read the sacred story.

THE ANGEL WITHDRAWN.

Gone is the angel whom I once called "Wife,"
    The sweet companion of my early years,
Who shared with me the griefs and joys of life,
    As hand in hand we trod this vale of tears,
      By mutual hopes inspired and undismayed by fears.

The one true friend on whom I could rely,
  Whose love was constant as the rolling sun
That never fails to light the morning sky
  And chase the shadows when the night is done,
  Which flee his presence and his glaring brightness shun.

My sole companion at all times was she,
  As I alone was her's from day to day ;
Contented in each other's presence we
  Could still rejoice, though clouds hung o'er our way,
  In quietude at home or where the squirrels play.

None other did her gentle heart desire
  Than my poor self ; I seemed to be her all,
My presence made her happiness entire,
  And none more loved upon this earthly ball
  Than I myself, by her who still my wife I call.

Together oft we did sweet counsel take,
  And talked of years we thought would yet be ours,
And nice arrangements for those years did make,
  As children on the sands build puny towers
  Unmindful of the waves and their destructive powers.

We, like the children, did our castles raise
  Upon the shifting sands or in the air,
To make provision for the future days
  We fondly hoped we might together share,
  Untroubled by distress and free from want and care.

But soon, alas ! the waves came tumbling in,
  And down the unsubstantial structures fell,
My dear was taken from this world of sin,
  With purer spirits worthily to dwell,
  Whose happy state of bliss no mortal tongue can tell.

And I was left behind to mourn her loss,
  And bear alone life's burden day by day,
To pine and grieve beneath the heavy cross.
  The dispensation did upon me lay,
  And walk in solitude life's now dull cheerless way.

Ah ! none can tell how keen is sorrow's pang,
　When parting from the friends we hold most dear,
On whom our joy's existence seems to hang.
　From morn till eve all thro' the changing year,
　But those who feel the smart and shed the bitter tear.

The nameless acts of kindness hourly shown,
　The nice attention to each little care,
The cheery word when one felt sad and lone ;
　The loving smile and fond expression there,
　Diffused glad joy around and comfort ev'rywhere.

Her dear companionship made home life sweet,
　The heart inspiring with her presence there ;
E'en when the storms upon our path might beat
　And we be weighted with a load of care,
　She ever hopeful was, nor yielded to despair.

If I was happy she would be content
　(Her happiness was locked within my own),
To give me pleasure her sweet life was spent ;
　And nought but gladness her own heart had known
　Had I been ever bright and more complacence shown.

If I was troubled she would be deprest
　(Her love was such she could not but be so)
Her kind solicitude was all confest.
　She ever sought to mitigate my woe
　And in unnumbered ways her love's devotion show.

Did pain or weariness my frame assail,
　Or disappointment mock my hoping heart,
Her love's true constancy did never fail
　To give relief and comfort to impart,
　Alleviate my pain and give my hope fresh start.

Did friends prove false and from me turn away,
　Did foes unite and 'gainst my peace conspire,
Did adverse circumstance claim me its prey
　And lead my steps into misfortune's mire ;
　Her kindness never flagged nor did her patience tire.

But on the contrary her love would then
   (As stars shine brighter when the night is dark,
Or trailing glow-worm in the lonely glen
    More clearly shows his phosphorescent spark),
    Be like a beacon light to guide my hapless bark.

The sweet contagion of her heart's content
   ·Diffused itself like richest fragrance there,
On those whose daily life with her was spent,
    And did the charms of dear presence share
    Which at all times would prove an antidote to care.

No affectation did her spirit know
   And no duplicity her speech reveal,
Her heart's true meaning in her face would show,
    As light or shade did o'er her features steal
    And with the force of words to other minds appeal.

Deceit nor guile her gentle nature knew,
   From all vindictive self-assertion free,
Both to herself and to her husband true ;
    Kind and attentive to her children she
    Who sadly miss her love and share their grief with me.

In her we had an Angel ever near,
   And knew it not until she had withdrawn,
When life at once looked dismal, dark and drear.
    At morn, at even, and at early dawn
    Her spirit having fled and her dear presence gone

To yonder radiant fields of light and bloom,
   In her own native element to soar,
Beyond the reach of earth's unrest and gloom,
    Beyond time's sea upon that unseen shore,
    To roam in pleasure there until we too pass o'er.

THE ANGEL'S RETURN.

Gone, did I say?   Her presence still is here,
   Although from sight and mortal sense withdrawn,
In spirit still she seemeth ever near,
   When daylight fades, or morning streaks the dawn,
   She has not left us quite nor altogether gone.

Still as of yore she round about us seems,
   Her kindly influence we still can feel :
Communicating with us in our dreams,
   Most vividly she doth herself reveal,
   Just as when in the flesh and not a whit less real.

One bright spring morning, as I dozing lay,
   Her mystic presence seemed within my room,
Which, for the time, did my whole being sway :
   Gone were night's shadows and the twilight's gloom,
   The now ascending sun proclaimed their certain doom.

Beside my bed her gentle figure stood
   Just as of old I saw her standing there,
I heard her voice as she in cheerful mood
   Did talk to me ; her loosely flowing hair   [fair.
   Adown her shoulders streamed, her shoulders white and

I knew not in my dream that she had died,
   My ignorance was then my joy and bliss ;
I felt quite sure that she was by my side,
   And in no other spirit sphere than this,
   As there she dressing stood, and nothing seemed amiss.

There in a semi-conscious state I lay,
   Not sound asleep nor was I quite awake,
But seemed entranced, as she in some strange way
   Did me control, and my fond fancy take,
   As in the days long gone for love immortal's sake.

And now as wishing to my waking sense
  To demonstrate the fact that she was there,
She gave me proof ere she departed thence,
  That what I saw was more than vision fair,
  That 'twas *her own real self* that did my chamber share.

She spoke to me, I opened then my eyes,
  And looking round she still was by my side ;
In rapt astonishment and sweet surprise
  At her I gazed ; then did she seem to glide
  And from my presence steal : I knew that she had died.

She faded from my sight, yet still I thought
  That though unseen she might be ever near :
My then experience most deeply wrought
  Within my soul, quelling each rising fear,
  That she, who long since dead, could thus to me appear.

Again, one quiet Sabbath afternoon,
  As I outstretched upon the sofa lay,
A drowsiness came on, and very soon
  I fell asleep, to dreams became a prey,
  And was again controlled in the broad light of day.

I scarce had entered sleep's sweet borderland,
  Its very threshold barely had I crossed,
Had but just yielded to its drowsy wand,
  And scarcely had my waking senses lost,
  (I was not then perturbed, I was not tempest-tost,)

When on the stairs light footsteps I did hear,
  Which most familiar to my sense did seem,
I most delighted was (I felt no fear
  No terrors did disturb my pleasant dream),
  My heart was full of joy, my happiness supreme.

She came into the room with pleasant smile,
  She entered freely by the open door.
She lightly tript with freedom's easy style,
  Just like herself, as in the days of yore
  When her own heart was light as mine had been before.

L

Unlike my former dream, this time I knew
  That she had long been absent from my sight,
And breaking thus on my astonished view,
  My spirit leapt with wonderful delight
  To see her thus again looking so smart and bright.

I rose to meet her as she drew me near,
  Advanced to clasp her with a kind embrace,
O'erjoyed to see her thus once more appear
  Just as of yore, in her accustomed place,
  The light of love and joy illumining her face.

But as her form I ventured to enfold,
  She disappeared and vanished from my sight ;
Her happy self no more I might behold,
  No more her countenance with love's delight
  Enraptured might I scan ; gone was her happy sprite.

Gone ? No, not gone, she still was very near,
  She had but hidden, though I knew not whence,
Concealed herself within the spirit sphere,
  Which oft impinges on the realms of sense,
  She was not far away although departed thence.

May it not be that worlds about us lie,
  Of whose existence we may nothing know,
And that our friends although unseen are nigh,
  And still much interest in earth-life show,
  Communicating thus to cheer us as we go ?

Matter to spirit is a thing of nought,
  And forms no barrier across its way,
Presents no obstacle to living thought ;
  With perfect freedom they can freely stray,
  Untramelled by its laws ; emancipated they.

From all its cramping limitations free,
  From world to world perhaps they come and go,
And oft when we suspect it not, may be
  In close attendance on their friends below,   [woe.
  To shield them with their love and cheer them in their

And all their earthly pilgrimage attend,
  Until like them they reach the other shore,
And altogether their glad voices blend ;
  Beyond time's sea, above its angry roar,
  For ever there to dwell with all their friends of yore.

THE MOTHER'S GRIEF.

Ah ! yes, bowed with grief at the thought of her loss ;
  Alas ! 'twas a poor little dead baby boy,
That ne'er saw the light and ne'er blessed the glad sight
  Of her who so anxiously waited her joy.

Ah ! yes, the dear Mother in anguish and grief,
  Borne up by the hope of a bright coming joy,
With labour and pain brought to birth once again,
  O ! sad disappointment ! a dead baby boy.

Ah ! yes, the sweet child found a premature grave,
  Which all the fond Mother's bright hopes did destroy ;
The bells of the earth never chimed at his birth,
  This little unfortunate dead baby boy.

Ah ! yes, he has gone and her loss she deplores,
  As children will grieve when they lose a fond toy,
Hopes cherished with pride, all at once dashed aside,
  Since Death ere the birth claimed the wee baby boy.

Ah ! yes, how she hoped she might bear him alive,
  Her heart all abrim with exuberant joy,
As close to her breast she would warmly have prest,
  The dear little stranger, the sweet baby boy.

L 2

Ah ! yes, and no doubt she could better have borne,
  The weakness that follows the birth of a boy,
If but her glad eyes could have seen the dear prize,
  All snugly beside her, a source of pure joy.

Ah ! yes, and I fancy she pictured the bliss,
  And thought of the happiness, pleasure and joy,
That shortly would be, when with pride she would see,
  And lovingly fondle her dear baby boy.

Ah ! yes, and she thought of the dear little girls,
  Who both would be pleased with a dear brother boy,
With whom they might play and to whom they might say,
  " Your coming has added so much to our joy."

Ah ! yes, and may be that she thought too of him,
  Who also might wish for a share in the joy,
Believing that he, as the father, would be,
  As proud as herself with a dear baby boy.

Ah ! yes, for she knew that he loved children well,
  And often would smile at their innocent joy,
Or grieve for the dears when he saw them in tears,
  And various comforting arts would employ.

Ah ! yes, this she knew and might, therefore, have thought,
  He too would rejoice at the birth of a boy,
Whose presence would bring like the birds of the spring,
  An increase of pleasure, contentment and joy.

Ah ! yes, but like Rachel, of whom we have read,
  And many fond mothers deprived of the joy,
Of bringing to birth amid gladness and mirth,
  A dear little treasure : a sweet baby boy.

Ah ! yes, she like these weeps because " he is not,"
  And grieves that grim Death should her hopes thus destroy,
That labour and pain have resulted again,
  In sorrow and sadness instead of bright joy.

Ah ! yes, Death has claimed him, as soon he will all,
  Whatever engagements their hands may employ ;
On the wide rolling earth whatever has birth,
  All ! all he will claim, as this poor baby boy.

A few weeks after the event referred to in the foregoing verses, the mother died very suddenly, of apoplexy, in the very height of the enjoyment of her (apparently) rapidly returning strength. She had been very happy all day, with her little girls, and had enjoyed very much every meal, particularly her tea. which was her last meal on earth.

She passed away just before the writer reached home, after having bidden her a most affectionate farewell (as usual) and leaving her in the best possible spirits in the morning. Her last words *to him* were :—"Good bye, my dear, I hope you'll get on all right," and waving her hand to him until he had passed out of her sight. But he never had the joy of seeing her again.

The verses that follow were written some time afterwards, their object being to show the bright side of this otherwise exceedingly dark and gloomy picture.

THE MOTHER'S JOY.

Ah ! yes, but though thus he was taken from her,
  She since hath rejoined him, her lost Angel boy,
In yon home afar where the glorified are,
  She shares with her babe in its unsullied joy.

Ah ! yes, she was taken one wild wintry eve,
  From darkness to light and from sorrow to joy,
O ! rapt'rous surprise caught up into the skies,
  Again to behold the sweet face of her boy.

Ah! yes, though we saw not the bright angel form,
    That took her sweet spirit to share its own joy,
We know that it came with pure love all aflame,
    And carried her home to her dear baby boy.

Ah! yes, she was taken and we left behind,
    In anguish to mourn for the loss of *our* joy ;
Her absence we grieve but rejoice to believe,
    That she is restored to her dear baby boy.

Ah! yes, caught away into regions of bliss,
    For ever to be with her dear baby boy,
For ever to share in the happiness there,
    Which nought can diminish and nothing destroy.

Ah! yes, and though she may never return,
    We hope that ere long we shall share in her joy,
The thought is most sweet that some day we shall meet,
    And see her again with her dear baby boy.

Ah! yes, and to worship with yonder bright throng,
    With all the redeemed our glad voices employ,
With sweet Seraphim and with pure Cherubin,
    And all heaven's host in the fulness of joy.

Ah! yes, with Apostles and Prophets to join,
    And Martyrs whose love the flames could not destroy,
The dungeon's dark shade, nor the axe make afraid,
    The presence of God was their strength and their joy.

Ah! yes, with all those who once lived on the earth,
    Whom foul persecution tried hard to destroy,
In caves and in dens amid mountains and glens,
    They hid from the fiends in the tyrant's employ.

Ah! yes, in the woods they would rather abide,
    In sheepskins and goatskins than part with their joy,
Some sawn through the bone, some to wild beasts were thrown,
    And *all* 'twas desired to betray and destroy.

Ah! yes, but they rest from their sufferings now,
    And share in the honour, the rapture and joy,
The Lord hath procured and for them hath insured,
    What no power on earth or in hell can destroy.

Ah! yes, they are resting, and rests my dear too,
  And shortly perhaps we may share in her joy,
The time may be nigh when my children and I,
  Shall join her again with her dear baby boy.

Ah! yes, praise the Lord we are lifting our heads,
  Redemption draws nigh that shall crown us with joy,
With Him we shall reign and our dear see again,
  His praises for ever our tongues shall employ.

Ah! yes, roll along then the time that remains,
  And hasten the day that shall perfect our joy,
When there we shall meet, cast our crowns at His feet,
  Myself, wife and daughters and dear baby boy.

IN MEMORIAM.

E. M. S.,

Died Dec. 24th, 1888.   In her Ninth year.

My darling, my treasure, my dear precious child,
  Alone and in anguish, I'm weeping for thee ;
It grieves me to think, O ! I shudder and shrink,
  That thou in the grave's cold oblivion should'st be.

My first-born, my Ethel, my sweet little girl,
  The joy and delight of my first wedded years,
The weight on my heart bids life's pleasures depart,
  My eyes are suffused with my grief and my tears.

Yes, dear Ethel Mary, my angel, my love,
  The thought of thy absence oppresses me sore,
No more thy sweet face may I kiss or embrace,
  Thy dear little form ; I shall see thee no more.

No more through the house will thy merry voice ring,
  No longer the hall shall resound with thy mirth ;
And never again, O ! the anguish and pain,
  When the spring shall return to gladden the earth,

Shall I, with thy dear little pet brother boy,
  Through the woods and the pines delightedly roam,
Where often before in those dear days of yore,
  We wandered with pleasure so near to our home.

Ah ! sweet happy times when with Gerald and thee,
  And all the delight of a fond mother's heart,
We gathered the flowers through the summer's glad hours,
  While lithe little squirrels would here and there dart,

In the trees overhead, and peep from behind,
  Just showing their ears and their bright little eyes ;
Then wildly and free to the top of the tree.
  Whose branches point up to the bright summer skies,

With a rustle and rush and peculiar cry,
  A note of alarm when disturbed in their glee,
Then out with a spring, and fast clutching they cling
  To the outstretching branch of the neighbouring tree.

While now from the distance another sound comes—
  "Tis neither a croak, nor a screech nor a song,
But a something between ; and looking is seen
  The black and white magpie a-skimming along,

Just over the tree-tops or down in between,
  Close followed by him, her companion and mate,
Who close by her side with affection and pride
  And constant devotion doth ever await.

Ah yes ! happy days, but my darling has gone,
  No more through the pine woods with her may we roam,
Laid by are her toys and departed our joys,
  The shadow of death has invaded our home.

O Death ! how relentless and cruel thou art !
  Compassion nor pity thy nature can feel,
Icy cold is thy clasp, unrelaxing thy grasp.
  Thou heed'st not our griefs, sure thy heart must be steel ;

Or no heart at all, but a framework of bones,
  Held together with nothing but sinew and skin :
Good Milton doth sing of thy darts and thy sting,
  The son and the offspring of ill-shapen Sin.

Dear Lady, take comfort, bewail not thy loss :
  Thy loss is thy little one's infinite gain,
O ! think of her now with the crown on her brow,
  'Twill soothe thy deep grief and lessen thy pain.

No longer suppose that thy daughter is dead,
  And lying alone in the dark dismal grave :
But lift up thine eyes to the bright glowing skies,
  For there with the noble, the good, and the brave,

Somewhere in the blue boundless regions of space,
  'Mong the orbs that encircle and lighten the earth,
The bright flashing stars, or on fiery red Mars,
  'Tis there with the Angels thy darling has birth.

Or further afield in the infinite depths,
  Where Science new wonders and glories reveals,
The grand " milky way " all ablaze with the day,
  (E'en now o'er my spirit their influence steals),

Where myriads of worlds through the telescope glow,
  All distinct and in order and subject to law,
That twinkle and shine with a radiance divine,
  Inspiring with wonder and worshipful awe,

And rapt adoration the spirit of man.
  Somewhere in the skies where no night ever falls,
With Angels of light, clad in garments of light,
  Thy dear little Ethel's sweet spirit now calls.

" Dear Parents weep not" (this her language must be),
  " For Jesus who reigns on yon' emerald throne,
" An Angel sent down with a robe and a crown,
  " And a message of love, He claimed me His own.

" So then do not weep or suppose I am lost,
  " I'm safe and at home with my Saviour and King,
" In the land of the blest, O sweet sacred rest !
  " Where glad hallelujahs triumphantly ring.

" And if I may know when the Angel is sent
  "(I think they will whisper the tidings to me),
" With message of love from these mansions above,
  "To thee my dear Mother, or Father, to thee :

" Or dear little Gerald or sweet baby boy,
  " I'll watch and I'll wait looking out with glad eyes,
" To see you appear and arrive safely here,
  " For ever to dwell in the bliss of the skies.

" For ever to worship our King and our God,
  " For ever with rapture His praises to sing ;
" For ever with me and my Saviour to be,
  " With loud acclamations these mansions shall ring.

" Till then my dear Mother and Father dear too,
  " And dear little Gerald and sweet baby boy.
" O ! grieve not for me I am happy and free.
  " Delightful my rest, everlasting my joy.

" Now, dear Mother, good bye, look up, do not cry,
  " Dear Father and Gerald and Baby farewell,
" For a brief little while then with peace and a smile.
  " Heaven's joys shall be yours and all will be well."

————————

MORTIMER,
BERKS.

DEAR MR. AND MRS. MOSDELL,

I feel I must write a line of thanks to you both for
the most kind sympathy you have shown to my husband
and me in our great sorrow. The poem in memory of our
dear child we shall certainly keep always, as a precious
relic, not only for the cleverness with which it is composed,
but for the true comfort and kindness which it expresses.

Only a loving and devoted mother can guess how very
sore my heart still is with the loss of our bright, happy little
Ethel, and the blank her absence makes in our home would
surely be unbearable if we did not feel quite certain of her
eternal happiness. I do like to think of our darling as
always a happy innocent child dwelling for ever in her

Heavenly Father's house, for ever free from sorrow, sin and pain, the only one of our children who is safe for ever. I must one day bring over and read to you some of the little stories and sermons she used to write for her own amusement, which are a great comfort to me now, as they show how truly she was one of Christ's little lambs. God was very merciful and took our pet very gently to Himself; she said she was "so tired," she wanted to go to Jesus. Dear little tired lamb, she is now at rest for ever.

With very many thanks again for the beautiful poem and sympathy,

I remain, yours truly,

M. E. S.

RURAL SECLUSION.

Away from the busy haunts of men,
　Away from the clam'ring cloud,
Away from the strife of city life,
Where fierce contentions all are rife,
　And men are vain and proud.

Away from the busy haunts of men,
　Away in the fruitful fields,
Where the golden grain that decks the plain,
Nurtured by sun and wind and rain,
　A bounteous harvest yields.

Away from the busy haunts of men,
　Away in the forest far,
Where soft winds blow and the flow'rets grow,
And murm'ring streamlets gently flow,
　And all things happy are.

Away from the busy haunts of men,
  Away on the mountains high,
Pure bracing air, where the prospect fair,
Stretches away so rich and rare,
  Beneath a boundless sky.

Away from the busy haunts of men,
  Away by the lonely shore,
Where the waves that beat low at our feet,
Proclaim in tones so softly sweet,
  The Power that we adore.

Away from the busy haunts of men,
  Away on the waters wide,
Where the zephyr sweeps while ocean sleeps
And Neptune nightly vigils keeps
  O'er all the flowing tide.

Away from the busy haunts of men,
  Away we delight to roam,
By silent shore or on lonely moor,
Or where the cat'racts rage and roar
  And watch their seething foam.

Away from the busy haunts of men,
  Away where the insects hum,
With a dreamy sound that doth resound,
Within the ear as round and round
  Continually they come.

Away from the busy haunts of men,
  Away with the squirrel free,
And the birds of song (a noble throng),
That pipe their music all day long
  Forth from the neighb'ring tree.

Away from the busy haunts of men,
  Away where the heather-bell
And wild flowers grow, that inspire us so,
And nature's purpose help to show
  On mountain or in dell.

Away from the busy haunts of men,
   Away we delight to go,
When morning shines or the day declines,
There where the woodbine wreathes and twines,
   And sweet wild roses grow.

Away from the busy haunts of men,
   Away where the woods proclaim,
In trees and flowers and rustic bowers,
The insects' hum and birds' sweet powers,
   Whence all their charms first came.

Away from the busy haunts of men,
   Away from low-thoughted care,
Where all around in each sight and sound,
Supreme enjoyment may be found,
   Which all alike may share.

Away from the busy haunts of men,
   Away from all human kind,
Where just for a while 'neath nature's smile,
The sad heart can its woes beguile
   And true contentment find.

Away from the busy haunts of men,
   Away where old Nature reigns,
In quietude and in solitude,
That suits the contemplative mood,
   And charms but never pains.

Away from the busy haunts of men,
   Away where all joyous things,
Wild, merry and free, cry out in their glee,
Trilling their glad notes from each tree.
   With which the woodland rings.

Away from the busy haunts of men,
   Away where divinely free,
The musing mind can employment find,
Catch inspiration from the wind
   And every spreading tree.

Away from the busy haunts of men,
　Away where the dead leaves fall,
With pleasing sound as they flutter round,
And everywhere upon the ground,
　Weave their own funeral pall.

Away from the busy haunts of men,
　Away from all vulgar joys,
Which leave behind but an aching mind,
While here we never fail to find
　Pleasure that never cloys.

Away from the busy haunts of men,
　Away from all discord there,
Where silence reigns and where peace obtains,
And over all its calm maintains,
　So sacred everywhere.

Away from the busy haunts of men,
　Away from the clam'ring crowd,
Away from the strife of city life,
Where fierce contentions all are rife,
　And men are vain and proud.

THE RETURN OF THE SWALLOWS.

The Swallows are soaring again in the sky,
　Rejoicing once more to be here,
From over the main they have come back again,
The insects to chase o'er the river and plain
　And tell us that summer is near.

That summer is near with its light and its joy,
   Its beauty of verdure and flowers,
Whose scent on the air is borne out ev'rywhere,
That all may delighted the rich fragrance share,
   So wondrously rife after showers.

From other fair climes to this isle of the sea,
   These birds of the wandering wing,
Their annual flight (instinct guides them aright),
Take over the waters to gladden our sight,
   And promise of better days bring.

Since last they departed and quitted our shores,
   What dark dreary days we have had :
Long nights, storm and rain, disappointment and pain.
Our hearts wrung with anguish again and again,
   But now we rejoice and are glad.

Although they had left us and gone far away,
   'Twas but for a brief little while,
Till winter should cease and the springtime of peace,
Spread over these latitudes and still increase,
   Transforming this ocean-girt isle.

They teach us a lesson we should not forget,
   But store it up well in the mind,
That though our joys fly and dark clouds fill the sky,
Like Swallows they all will return by-and-bye,
   When we life's true purpose shall find.

Ah ! yes, and our friends who have passed out of sight,
   Whose presence no longer we view,
On some other shore we shall see them once more,
And oh ! how delightful the converse of yore,
   With rapture we then shall renew.

     May 7th, 1890.

TENNYSON'S "IN MEMORIAM."

O! sweetly plaintive "In Memoriam,"
  So full of pity and of tenderness,
  Of human sympathy and gentleness,
That I in love with its dear Author am.

A pure affection breathes in all its lines,
  A strong deep yearning t'wards our sorrowing race :
  The shadows of our tragic life we trace,
But over all triumphantly " Hope " shines.

The " Larger Hope " which of late years evolved
  More clearly and more plainly than before,
  Revealing Him our God Who heretofore
In " Dante's dark Inferno " all unsolved,

A King unmerciful, of love bereft,
  In terror reigning o'er the men He made,
  Compelling them through sorrows deep to wade,
And in Himself no good or pity left.

Enshrouding all in universal gloom,
  And blotting out the fair celestial light ;
  No cheering radiance left to bless the sight
Of man who blindly staggers to his doom.

" All hope abandon ye who enter here,"
  O'er those forbidding gloomy portals hung ;
  While through its hollow dismal chambers rung
The agonizing accents of despair.

Cimmerian darkness and primeval shade,
  Nor faintest gleam of all-sustaining hope,
  Through endless ages there condemned to grope,
By Him Who all the fair creation made.

O false 'Theology, and cruel as false,
  A libel on that all-embracing love
  Which from supernal, sacred heights above
Doth lighten e'en the nether world's dark vaults.

Love universal, boundless as the space,
  Where mighty planets in their grandeur roll,
  And flaming comets rush from pole to pole,
The outlet of the mind, God's dwelling place.

Revealing Him, our Father, thus once more,
  The vision of our earliest tend'rest years,
  Whose all pervading-presence calmed our fears,
And did our faith and confidence restore.

O fertile Fancy, and creative Brain,
  O Sacred Genius, noble and refined ;
  O God-like spirit, consecrated mind,
O Temple pure, and Virtue's heavenly train !

Dear Tennyson, thy hallowed Poem lifts
  The musing mind of him who reads its page
  Above himself ; beyond this grov'lling age
To where heaven's crystal light in purest rifts,

Beams gladly on this dark benighted world :
  (Like Angels from the sinless regions sent,
  And pointing upwards whence they came and went),
The clouds roll by, the skies are all unfurled,

A flood of light now rushes on the mind,
  Peace takes possession of the human soul,
  Though lightnings flash or distant thunders roll,
God reigns supreme, and He is good and kind.

O happy frame of mind, O blissful state
  Of him who leans on heaven's all-gracious King !
  He can rejoice in hope, and he can sing,
Though hell's dark forms about his pathway wait.

Though adverse circumstances girt him in,
  And all the world against him seem to rise,
  With anchor firmly grappled to the skies,
He heeds them not, nor fears the powers of sin.

M

O ! may this glad estate be ever mine,
    Of walking close to God while here on earth,
    'Till life shall cease and I in heaven have birth ;
And may it, friend, be also ever thine.

Dear Laureate ! thy elevating page,
    Thy fervent grief and longing most intense,
    For that dear absent form (O sad suspense !)
Do now my pencil and my thoughts engage.

In mournful numbers and sweet plaintive song,
    That dear friend's absence thou dost pine and grieve,
    Death did thee of thy best beloved bereave,
Thy grief is, therefore, lasting, deep and strong.

But bravely and with patience thou dost bear
    The lot thy God hath measured out for thee,
    Rejoicing even in thy grief that he
Thy much loved Arthur basks in radiance there.

Where in that other and that better life
    The pure in heart who ever seek the light,
    Behold with rapture that all-glorious sight—
The face of God.   Sweet alleluiahs rife.

While Angels their bright golden lyres attune,
    With light ineffable the region glows,
    From heart to heart immortal gladness flows,
O sacred joy, O everlasting noon !

From thy devoted and heroic book
    May we true fortitude and wisdom learn ;
    In all our sorrows and our griefs discern
Heaven's purpose ; and onward, upward look :

Believing sure (for 'tis by faith we go,
    We have to trust where now we cannot see,
    Like ships in darkness out upon the sea,
That watch and wait the morning's ruddy glow)

That God our Father loves His children well,
    Nor doth afflict us with a blind caprice,
    But that we may attain more lasting peace,
And evermore in His dear presence dwell.

Dear gifted Poet, reluctantly adieu,
  I'd gladly linger musing still with thee,
  Thy muse my own exalts, I feel more free
Since having read thy sweetest poem through.

Farewell thou man of worth and honoured years !
  "Till thou thy Arthur once again shalt see,
  "Till death my fetters breaks and I am free,
And we have passed beyond this vale of tears,

To that dear home where loved ones meet again,
  Long interrupted friendships are restored,
  Joy reigns supreme and God is all adored,
Beyond the reach of sorrow, care and pain.

OCTOBER 10TH, 1890.

To Mrs. Moore.

Full thirteen times the lunar lamp hath lighted,
  With silver rays this sublunary sphere,
Since last my muse, instructed and delighted,
  Invoked a blessing on each coming year,
  That might remain to thee and thy loved consort here.

And once again I beg to be permitted
  To give expression to my heart's goodwill,
Now that another shortlived year has flitted,
  With its vicissitudes of good and ill
  Into the mighty past ; by it made greater still.

Nought else I trust but joy and radiant gladness,
  Have been thy lot through all the changing year,
That no disturbing element of sadness
  Hath marr'd thy bliss, or caused the crystal tear
  To glisten in thine eye or on thy cheek appear :

M 2

But that thy way hath even been more cheerful
　Than were the blissful days that went before,
That nought hath happen'd which could make thee fearful,
　Like that grim thought which troubled thee of yore
　And which I fain would pray may harass thee no more.

But if it should again, thy soul distressing,
　Yield not to fear nor give thy heart to grief,
Within what seems a curse may lurk a blessing
　Beyond imagination or belief,
　(Though pain be sharp it cannot but be brief)
　And greater be the joy when comes the glad relief.

The God Who spreads the glowing skies above thee,
　Is thine Almighty and thy constant friend,
And He Who changeth not doth ever love thee
　From life's beginning even to its end ;
　On Him thou mayest, therefore, at all times depend.

Although from us at times His way is hidden,
　And we may fail His wondrous path to trace,
O ! be it ours to do as we are bidden,
　Believe His word which promises all grace,
　Shall unto us be given whatever be our case.

The Great " I Am " is He, Who ever liveth,
　The soul of all that is or e'er can be,
He is life's source and unto all life giveth ;
　" In Him all live and move " and therefore we
　Should ever trust e'en when no guiding light we see.

Upon the winds in majesty He rideth,
　Or through the deep His awful way He takes ;
He also with the pure in heart abideth
　And *there* His constant habitation makes,
　Diffusing light and joy as He love's secrets breaks.

How sweet to know that He Who holds the waters
　Within the hollow of His mighty hand,
Will thus reside with earth's frail sons and daughters
　And hold communion with His faithful band,
　Who, scattered thro' the world, are found in every land.

This wondrous globe by Him is kept in motion,
  And never fails nor halts in its career ;
Each continent, each island and each ocean,
  The myriad forms of life that there appear,
  Are borne unceasing onwards round the central sphere.

And still more mighty orbs are ever sweeping,
  In graceful circles thro' the realms of space,
And all unfailing perfect order keeping,
  None ever swerving from its law-bound place,
  Where they their courses run as in eternal race.

The "milky way" where worlds unnumbered rolling,
  Which scatter far and wide the shades of night,
Are all His work and under His controlling ;
  Fountains are they of never-failing light,
  And witness as they shine to their Creator's might.

While far beyond where proud but puny Science
  Can pierce with keen and telescopic eye,
May *other* systems rise which give defiance
  To all attempts their distance to descry,
  By mortal man while scanning the nocturnal sky.

O ! none can tell how wide is His creation,
  What wonders roll within the vast profound,
All for our happy future contemplation,
  When we no longer by earth-ties are bound,
  Its limits then perhaps we may explore and sound.

From world to world thro' mighty spaces ranging,
  Beyond the Solar Orb our flight extend,
'Mid scenes of grandeur that for ever changing
  Shall sweet enchantment to the spirit lend,
  As thro' infinity our rapturous way we wend.

The Stars He names and all their number telleth,
  Yet to the earth a gracious eye He bends,
With lowly contrite ones He ever dwelleth ;
  Calls them not servants but His chosen friends
  And all their pilgrim way with watchful care attends.

The sum of all is this He is our *Father*,
  And in His hands we passively would rest ;
Come sorrow or come joy we yet would rather
  In patience lean upon His faithful breast,
  Reposing sweetly there we cannot but be blest.

And if the children of so great a Being,
  We must ourselves be greater than we think,
When peaceful Death our happy spirits freeing,
  And we shall stand upon life's awful brink,
  Our souls' true nature then will us with Angels link.

May this sweet thought at all times ever cheer thee,
  While thou shalt here and in the flesh remain,
That Christ the Lord Himself is ever near thee,
  To soothe life's anguish and to ease its pain
  And whisper words of hope whene'er thy joys shall wane.

Thy Pilot He upon life's surging ocean,
  And o'er its waters thy frail barque will bring ;
Calm and serene amidst tumultuous motion
  And angry elements thy soul can sing,   [King.
  Knowing that winds and waves own Him their Lord and

Though rocks abound and breakers rise before thee,
  Safe through them all the vessel He will guide ;
Though black as night the heavens lour o'er thee
  And dangers threaten thee on ev'ry side,
  Yet be thou not afraid but still in Him confide.

The skies shall clear, the tempest cease its raging,
  The howling winds shall all be lulled to sleep,
And peaceful scenes thy gladden'd eyes engaging
  In happy ecstacy thy soul shall keep,
  Till heaven's fair port is gained beyond the rolling deep.

Rely alone on Him and like a river,
  Both full and deep thy peace shall ever flow,
With cheerful mind acknowledge Him the Giver
  Of all the mercies that He doth bestow,
  And *greater* blessings yet thy constant heart shall know.

VENUS, AS EVENING STAR.

Beautiful star, in space afar,
  Bright, flaming to the sight,
A living gem and diadem
  Upon the brow of night.

If all day long dark storm-clouds throng,
  And then the skies should clear,
Thy brilliant form behind the storm
  Serenely doth appear.

Above the care and dark despair
  The anguish and the woe,
The silent tears, the hopes and fears
  That mortals feel and know.

Above the noise of vulgar joys,
  Above the world's wild din,
The clash of arms, the rude alarms,
  The darkness and the sin.

Above the strife of earthly life,
  Above the battle plain,
Its hollow moans and mournful groans,
  Its dying and its slain.

Above the reach of human speech,
  The mandates of earth's kings,
Their valiant sons, their ships and guns,
  And all war's puny things.

Above the sea so wild and free,
  The elements at war,
The surging waves, the wind that raves,
  While both in tumult are.

Above the moon (the sailor's boon)
  That waxes and that wanes ;
As through the skies she nightly flies,
  Lighting earth's vales and plains.

In lucid beams thy glory streams
    Upon the earth below,
On India's land, on Afric's sand,
    And on the polar snow.

The rolling deep where tempests sweep,
    The ever heaving main,
A mirror seems wherein thy beams
    And all the starry train

Reflected are.   Each single star,
    There scintillates and shines,
And glints and glows in calm repose,
    Between the waves' dark lines.

Thy parallax and shifting tracks,
    Around the orb of day,
As year by year thy rolling sphere
    Owns his more potent sway.

Sometimes as now on heaven's brow
    When rosy day declines,
In flaming car as evening star,
    Calm and serenely shines.

Sometimes thy ray at break of day
    Precedes the rising sun,
Beaming afar as morning star
    When twilight has begun.

Thus thou dost change thy place, and range
    The blue nocturnal space,
Around the sun dost ever run
    Thy interesting race.

To mortal man, his life a span,
    How wonderful art thou,
Through countless years thy disc appears
    Adorning heaven's brow.

Thy wondrous age earth's wisest sage
    With all that crams his brain,
Of nature's laws, and nature's cause,
    Nor knows nor can explain

Why, whence or where, so passing fair,
  Thy origin, thy date,
And whither tends, or whither ends,
  And what shall be thy fate.

Unnumbered years of smiles and tears
  Have dawned and rolled away,
Since mortals here first saw thy sphere,
  Beheld its cheering ray.

But long before those days of yore,
  Thou lovely brilliant star,
Thy course began, thy circuit ran,
  Immeasurably far.

Ages untold, wondrously old,
  Yet always seeming new,
So pure and clear thou dost appear,
  Each time thy form I view.

Compared with thee what worms are we !
  How brief our earthly stay !
How little know as on we go
  The creatures of a day.

Convincing sign of power divine :
  The Hand that hung thee there,
Thy orb sustains and ever reigns
  Through nature everywhere.

Creation sings, with music rings
  The starry vault of night ;
The worlds of space, each in his place,
  Chant the Creator's might.

THE NEW HYMN.

Words by W. H. Payne.   Music by H. T. Hart.

———

DEAR SIR,

    I beg to thank you
    For your new "Christmas Hymn,"
I've read it through and sung it too,
    In thankfulness to Him,

Who moved you to indite it,
    The spirit that inspired,
The musing mind sweet thoughts to find,
    And heavenly ardour fired.

I like the Hymn immensely,
    The genius much admire,
That in the lines so clearly shines,
    With true poetic fire.

The *music* is refreshing,
    So simple yet sublime,
Well suited to the piece all through
    In measure and in time.

I do congratulate you
    On your new Christmas Song,
And pray success its course may bless,
    And waft it well along.

And when our earthly journey,
    Our pilgrimage shall cease,
May I and you and dear Hart too
    'Mid Heaven's perfect peace,
Where "Angels soaring, hosts adoring,"
Songs and alleluiahs pouring
    And joys that still increase,
May we together sing "The song
    "Of Moses and the Lamb."

The words recall the message
  The song the Angels sang,
When from the skies with sweet surprise
  The heavenly music rang.

The Shepherds there abiding,
  On Judah's starlit plains,
Look'd up amazed, with rapture gazed,
  To hear the wondrous strains :

Which, floating through the welkin,
  And gently borne along,
Broke softly there, the startled air,
  A sweet Angelic song.

A strange unearthly vision,
  Of Angels pure and bright,
Those men then saw and filled with awe
  They trembled with affright.

But, list'ning to the Anthem,
  In heaven's own native tongue,
These frightened men grew calm again,
  So sweet the Angels sung.

" Fear not ye trembling mortals,
  "Glad tidings do we bring,
" A Saviour's name we now proclaim,
  "His advent 'tis we sing ;

"To you in David's township,
  " Is born this very day,
" In lowly shed, on manger bed,
  "Where peaceful cattle lay,

"The long foretold Messiah ;
  " The Prince of Peace and Light ;
" Whose kingdom will extend until
  " All nations feel the might,

" Of gentle, soft persuasion,
  " And kind, forgiving love,
" Till *all* return, nor longer spurn,
  "The message from above.

" All glory in the highest,
  " To Him our God and King ";
Thus cherubim and seraphim,
  In unison did sing.

" And on the earth be gladness,
  " Goodwill to *all* we bring,
" And lasting peace that ne'er shall cease,"
  Thus did the Angels sing.

The message now unfolded,
  The Angel hosts retire,
Back to the skies, with rapture rise,
  On wings of flaming fire.

O ! sweet enchanting story,
  Sung by the Angel throng,
And long foretold, by Seers of old,
  In canticle and song.

We heard it in our childhood,
  Beside our Mother's knee.
And still revere, it grows more dear,
  No sweeter song can be.

Their theme was Man's Redemption,
  Let us take up the strain,
In songs of praise *our* voices raise,
  Till we their joys attain.

Till we in heaven's glory,
  With Angels shall unite,
Through endless days to sing His praise,
  With rapture and delight.

PRIVATION.

Wintry winds around us raving,
  Snowflakes whit'ning all the ground,
Poverty its hardships braving,
Helpless want assistance craving,
  Where, O ! where, can help be found.

Cheerful fires and food are needed
  (What is home where these are not ?)
Let privation's cry be heeded,
Let her wants be all conceded,
  Brighten up her dismal lot.

Little children pale and shoeless,
  And their faces pinched with want,
Older countenances hueless,
Oft are seen (though sometimes viewless)
  Bony forms with hunger gaunt.

They our sisters are and brothers,
  There the stamp divine we trace,
Fathers they and anxious Mothers,
Not to us but unto others,
  Members of one common race.

They our kin and blood relations,
  This fact all should recognise,
Not contemn their lowly stations,
Nor despise their avocations,
  Neither disregard their cries.

Creatures all of circumstances
  (This should too be borne in mind),
They perhaps had lesser chances,
Than their fellows which enhances
  Much their claims on human kind.

In the slums of every city,
   Wretchedness and want appear,
Sights that move the heart to pity
(Oft described in humble ditty),
   Starting on its course the tear.

Round about their path temptation,
   Ever waits as for his prey,
Evil's sure contamination,
With much baleful emulation,
   Spreads infection night and day.

At this time of mirth and pleasure,
   When the horn of plenty pours,
Rich abundance without measure,
Bringing us much joy and leisure,
   Spurn not those who at our doors

Ask an alms or food desiring,
   Or a drop of water crave,
Kindly we their state enquiring,
With some comfort them inspiring,
   Give them counsel good and brave.

Let our motives be transparent,
   Be our sympathy sincere,
Let our goodwill be apparent,
To the vicious and the arrant,
   Should such at our doors appear.

Just for once their sad hearts cheering,
   What we give we shall not miss,
Charity with grace appearing,
Given freely without fearing,
   Shall add pleasure to our bliss.

Christmas, 1890.

THE LATE SIR PAUL HUNTER.

A tribute of respect.

Mortimer mourns its foremost son to day,
Its people grieve to see the lifeless clay
　　Borne down the village street,
To yonder quiet churchyard burial ground,
Where the turf, in many a sacred mound,
　　Their sorr'wing gaze doth meet.

Vast numbers throng their sympathy to show,
With those bereft and sunk in depths of woe,
　　And true respect to pay
To him whose body lies in death's embrace :
('The final lot of all our mortal race),
　　Who gave now takes away.

In him the poor have lost a constant friend,
To them he oft did consolation send
　　When they were in distress ;
And round his silent grave they gather now,
Sincere their grief as reverently they bow,
　　His memory they will bless.

Though they were poor they *now are poorer* still,
Deprived of him, his friendship and good will,
　　His word of kindly cheer ;
With those less favour'd he would share his wealth,
And ever did his gen'rous acts by stealth,
　　Nor let them once appear.

His honour'd name for many years hath been
A household word, where he was daily seen,
　　The life and soul of all ;
'Twould hang familiar upon ev'ry tongue,
The aged did esteem him ; and the young
　　Rejoiced to see Sir Paul.

His well-known residence upon the " Hill,"
Where he so long life's duties did fulfil,
   Stands like a lighthouse there ;
From whence did radiate on life's dark sea,
Love's beacon light, sad, lonely hearts to free
   From darkness and despair.

A Christian gentleman, such was our friend,
Painless and peaceful was his sudden end ;
   Twin Angels, sleep and death,
His chamber enter'd and around him spread
Their "downy pinions," and his spirit fled,
   Where life is not a breath.

All classes here will miss his genial face ;
A quiet sadness seems to fill the place
   Where he so long was known ;
Death's gloomy shadow like a fun'ral pall,
Rests on his home and thence extends to all ;
   All now feel sad and lone.

May those who thus such heavy loss sustain,
Have faith in God, till they shall meet again,
   That "all things work for good";
That he whose absence they so much deplore
Has been translated to a brighter shore
   Beyond death's swelling flood.

January, 1890.

                    MORTIMER HILL,
                      MORTIMER.

MR. MOSDELL.

    I thank you most sincerely for the touching verses
on the death of my very dear husband ; it is a great
comfort to me in my great sorrow to see how he was
respected and beloved by all in the village he loved so
well.

              Yours faithfully,
                CONSTANCE HUNTER.

THE LARK BEFORE DAYLIGHT.

February 9th, 1889.

———

O list to the lark as she mounts up aloft,
  While darkness and daylight together contest,
Nor night nor yet day but the twilight's soft ray,
  That wakens the world from its slumber and rest.

High up overhead in the dim growing light,
  A musical melody falls on my ear,
The lark greets the day with a cheerful glad lay,
  That's perfectly ravishing only to hear.

Yes, only to hear, for she cannot be seen,
  The shadows of night linger yet in the sky;
But up she has gone at the first streak of dawn,
  And well do we know that the lark is on high.

We know she is there, although lost to our view,
  The music the singer's sweet presence reveals,
The wild welkin rings with the song that she sings,
  Which over my senses delightfully steals.

With rapture I listen, as upwards I gaze,
  And try to discover the source of the song,
Which loudly and clear breaks so sweet on my ear,
  Bewitchingly lovely, enchantingly long.

The lark loves the morning, nor waits for the light,
  But rises ere darkness gives place to the day;
And up on her wings, oh! how sweetly she sings
  Her artlessly simple inspiriting lay.

The stars are yet shining, the world is asleep,
  But soaring aloft in the clear spreading blue,
Singing loudly and long a grand "sightless song"
  The lark tries to waken and cheer the world too.

N

THE BIRDCATCHER.

From an unfinished piece on " Birds."

How oft from the slums of the city or town,
  With lime and with traps and dead birds to decoy
The feathery race from their own native place,
  Rough men wander forth to ensnare or destroy.

Or sometimes with *live* birds secured to the cage,
  That twitter and call to the birds in the air,
Who quickly appear unsuspectingly near,
  And shortly the captive's captivity share.

They enter the cage through the wide open door
  (Sweet innocent creatures no danger they see),
The "Catcher" close by with a keen eager eye,
  Is watching their movements.   A base man is he.

Or sometimes their little feet press on the lime,
  The lime with such fast sticking properties fraught,
The poor little things struggle hard with their wings,
  And try to get free, but alas ! they are caught.

Thus many sweet songsters stoop down to their fate,
  Stuck fast in the lime or entrapped in the cage,
Where closely confined (how extremely unkind),
  With nothing their anguish to sooth or assuage.

Then homewards these unfeeling creatures return,
  Their cages well stocked with a sweet singing throng,
Whose cheerful glad lays in the summer's bright days,
  The woodland's wild echoes had waked loud and long.

O hard-hearted wretches we envy you not,
  No touch of soft pity your nature can feel,
Not e'en for the bird whose sweet songs you have heard,
  From yonder green covert delightedly steal.

Ah ! dear little prisoners, victims of war,
　Of war waged unjustly, unsparingly too,
By men of low mind and depraved human kind,
　Who try without labour to live upon you.

And how little they think, these rough brutal men,
　When home with their innocent captives they go,
To the alleys or courts, their fav'rite resorts,
　Dark dens all unsuited to wild birds we know.

How little they think of the suff'ring they cause,
　To those that they take and the birds that are left,
How they languish and pine a sure certain sign,
　That keenly they realise they are bereft.

The brighter their plumage, the sweeter their song,
　The more do these villains their capture desire,
The more eagerly ply their low craft and try
　To make them their own little captives entire.

But O ! how they lessen the music of earth,
　The grand lyric music that nature supplies,
The birds little throats pour a torrent of notes,
　That floods both the earth and the wide spreading skies.

The Bullfinch, the Chaffinch, the sweet Linnet too,
　With notes all distinctive and notes all their own,
Of all the bird throng each one sings his own song,
　'Tis nature's distinction by which they are known.

And other wild songsters whose ravishing lays,
　We often have heard with such rapture and joy,
Whose grand music trills o'er the dales and the hills,
　These, these are the birds they ensnare and destroy.

I often have wondered when meeting these men,
　Why 'tis that they thus are permitted to go,
Why 'tis that the laws don't espouse the birds' cause
　And round them protection *more stringently* throw.

N 2

THE BIRD DEALER.

Reply to a Lady Correspondent.

All honour to her who with pencil or pen,
The cause of the birds has espoused once again.
   By writing a few kindly verses ;
In which she depicts with a feeling we share,
How "dealers" will torture the birds of the air,
   Their base "dealing" tricks she rehearses.

"Nine birds sometimes die out of twelve that are bought,"
By him of the "Catcher" who first the birds caught,
   With lime and with traps and with cages ;
Where robb'd of the freedom they had in the sky,
And huddled together no wonder they die,
   No wonder the poor "Dealer" rages.

His losses are great, though we pity *him* not,
But think he deserves all the trouble he's got,
   'Tis only the *birds* that we pity ;
Decoy'd from their homes by these low cunning men,
They *steal* them themselves from the woodland and glen,
   Then *sell* to the man in the city.

They know by some means how to keep them alive,
To make them look well and *apparently* thrive,
   And tickle their throats into singing :
Until they can sell them to him who has got
More money than sense (such is some people's lot),
   A lucrative trade to them bringing.

And now he has got them the birds droop and pine,
Their eyes lose their lustre no longer they shine ;
   No longer wild melodies pouring
In musical cadence and ravishing notes,
Delightful to hear from their sweet little throats,
   As when in the sky they were soaring.

'Tis now the confinement they still have to bear,
Deprived of the freedom they had in the air,
    Where they in sweet liberty flying,
Doth make them to languish, they fall in the cage,
They die broken-hearted with nought to assuage,
    Their agonies when they are dying.

Dear innocent creatures the true friends of man,
Ye make life as cheerful for us as ye can,
    And this is how base man repays ye ;
He robs ye of freedom, your music he stills,
By painful degrees he your precious life kills,
    He slowly and cruelly slays ye.

A most "needless slaughter" she rightly asserts,
The "Dealer," of course, has but got his deserts,
    We hope the vile "Catcher" doth share them ;
They both are engaged in the same lazy trade,
By which *without work* sometimes livings are made,
    'Tis, therefore, but right we should pair them.

I trust the good Lady whose verses I read,
Will also read mine and see what I have said,
    We both are as one in this matter ;
Between us the "Catcher," the "Dealer" as well,
Have been roughly handled (our verses will tell),
    The former no less than the latter.

A bird she herself is *in name* without wings,
'Tis, therefore, most fitting the verses she sings,
    A kind heart I'm sure she possesses ;
A heart to forgive me that which I now say,
The freedom I take with her name thus to play,
    The *Wren* evermore each bird blesses.

THE RETURN OF THE SWALLOWS.

Again in the heavens the Swallows are seen,
  Foretelling the pleasures the summer will bring,
High up in the sky O! how graceful they fly,
  And O! too how long they remain on the wing.

With joy we behold them returned to our shores,
  And gladly a warm hearty welcome extend,
From over the sea their old friends come to see,
  And with us their summer vacation to spend.

Ah! birdies, I wonder if ever ye think,
  When back from that far distant country ye fly,
Of those whom ye left and whose hearts were bereft,
  As they watched you depart with half moistened eye,

To those sunny regions far over the sea,
  And out of the reach of the frost and the snow,
Where each rolling year as the winter draws near,
  'Tis nature's arrangement the Swallows should go.

If ever ye think of those dear absent friends,
  Who watch and who wait as the spring draweth nigh,
How intensely they yearn to see you return,
  Serenely to bathe in their own native sky.

And to build 'neath the gable, or under the eaves,
  Or snugly ensconced 'neath the low hanging thatch,
In the barn or the shed just up overhead,
  A place where to sleep and your little ones hatch.

A little mud nest built with wonderful skill,
  And infinite patience and labour and toil,
Which when thou hast done, in mere mischief or fun,
  Rude ignorant hands will sometimes despoil.

But still all undaunted, again thou dost try,
  To make thee a home where to tarry and rest,
From the side of the pond, or clay hills beyond,
  Whichever may seem to thy fancy the best ;

The mud from the lane or the pool in the street,
  'Tis thence thou obtainest thy building supplies,
Whichever sticks best is I fancy the test,
  When exposed to the heat of hot sultry skies.

Thus little by little and still plodding on,
  From morning till eve while thy tiny house grows,
So tight the mud sticks as each piece thou dost fix,
  All strong and secure, as a bird only knows.

And now having used all the mud in thy beak
  (Ye have no attendants to labour for you),
Away thou dost fly for a further supply,
  And quickly returnest thy toil to renew.

'Twas nature that taught thee to build thy own house,
  (As instinct doth guide thee across the blue sea),
Nor mortar nor bricks but with mud that fast sticks,
  Thou buildest thy cottage as neat as can be.

Half basin the shape with a neat little hole,
  Which serves as a doorway and window as well,
In which the light streams when the glad morning beams,
  O'er woodland and river, on mountain and dell.

In comfort and safety ye there may abide,
  Up out of the reach of your friends and your foes,
A pretty retreat from the sun's scorching heat,
  And where both may enjoy your well-earned repose.

Thus happy all day with thy consort and mate,
  And loving and peaceful all through the still night.
Together ye dwell in your neat little cell,
  Completely shut in from the world's vulgar sight.

There all unmolested by want or distress,
  Untroubled by losses or cankering care,
A picture of bliss in a world such as this,
  Exceedingly seldom and painfully rare.

The fruits of affection and nuptial delight,
  In embryo form and enclosed in a shell,
Together ye tend, while your purposes blend,
  In mutual concord together ye dwell.

From morning till evening one keeps the eggs warm,
  From evening till morning the fond mother sits,
With wonderful care and with patience so rare;
  While cheerfully, lovingly, to and fro flits,

Her constant companion, who all the day long,
  With am'rous devotion so faithful and true,
On love's willing wings continually brings,
  Supplies of fresh food for himself and her too.

How oft in the summer before I am up,
  The sunshine a-streaming my chamber into,
While lying awake from the early daybreak,
  As sometimes when wakeful I happen to do;

How oft on the window or closely drawn blind
  (When happens thy nest to be just up above),
Thy pleasing form flits while thy gentle bride sits
  And sweetly to her thou dost twitter thy love.

Thus day after day kindly cared for and fed,
  By him who delights in attending to thee.
The time glides away and brings on the glad day,
  The day that ye both are so anxious to see.

And now in the nest what excitement appears,
  What happiness there in that little house reigns,
What bursting of shells, O! the joy that it tells,
  The mother bird reaps the reward of her pains.

O! auspicious morning, eventful glad day,
  A sweet little progeny now there appears;
One, two, three and four and sometimes even more,
  To people the sky in the on-coming years.

O! how the fond mother broods over her charge,
  And spreads out her feathers to keep them all warm,
Not one of her pets the kind parent forgets,
  But covers them all and protects them from harm.

She does not desert them or leave them alone,
  As some wretched mothers their offspring forsake,
And leave them to cry or to perish and die,
  The thought makes the heart of the tender to ache.

But like the kind mother devoted and true,
　With all the affection that nature supplies,
All day and all night 'tis her constant delight,
　To be with her young and attend to their cries.

But when they are grown and the feathers appear,
　For a brief little while she quits her young brood,
Up into the skies in pursuit of the flies,
　Which constitute chiefly her principal food.

But quickly returning to her happy cot,
　That little mud dwelling up under the eaves,
Those dear little things with soft beaks and small wings,
　And all their bird troubles at once she relieves.

The food that she brings they all gladly partake,
　Their little mouths open tremendously wide,
So much so in fact if they only were pack'd,
　I fear 'twould be said that "the birdies all died."

And now having supp'd they at once nestle down,
　The mother again spreads about them her wings,
And soundly they sleep while the parent birds keep
　A long loving watch o'er the dear little things.

Their duties henceforth are to feed and to guard,
　The dear little family nature has sent,
To screen them from harm and protect from alarm,
　And in their defence their own lives must be spent.

O ! how the birds thrive and how strong they all get,
　How rapidly each little Swallow does grow,
They'll soon quit the nest, fly aloft like the rest,
　And over the blue distant waters will go.

Already they get by the doorway and look,
　Or climb to the window (they both are but one),
Their bright little eyes peer up into the skies,
　Where glows and where flashes the grand summer sun.

Their tiny white throats and their little black heads,
　All huddled together so eager to see,
One, two, three and four, peeping out from the door,
　And looking so innocent down upon me.

But O ! what a twitter at once they all make,
　What can be the cause of this sudden outcry ?
How loudly they call, O ! I fear they will fall,
　They stretch out their necks as if they would fly

And looking around to discover the cause,
　Two Swallows I notice draw lovingly near,
Now high and now low, then off again go,
　My presence I think it must be that they fear.

I, therefore, retire to a more distant spot,
　And watch them as instantly back they return,
To the quick-sighted brood all clam'ring for food,
　And *now* I the cause of the outcry discern.

They do not give back as the parents approach,
　But still throng and press at the window or door,
A row of bright eyes and beaks all the same size,
　Their little feet pressing upon the mud floor.

The old bird has, therefore, to cling to the side,
　Hang unto the wall as she best knoweth how,
While her offspring she feeds with gnats, flies, or seeds,
　Or whatever else she may choose to allow.

But O ! what a flutter and craning of necks,
　And gaping of beaks for the food that is brought,
Direct from the skies where the mother bird flies,
　And chases the insects until they are caught.

O ! what a sweet picture, how loving they seem,
　How pleasantly life with the Swallows must go,
High up in the nest O ! how safely they rest,
　And nothing but happiness surely they know.

Up under the roof in their neat little home,
　All through the dark night, O ! how snug they can be
No harm need they fear for no foes can come near,
　And nought can disturb them, the Swallows are free.

Their house is their own since they built it themselves,
　And, therefore, they pay no exorbitant rent,
But happy and free as the birds in the tree,
　Their lives daily pass in the sweetest content.

O ! how interesting the Swallows appear,
   When closely observed with intelligent eye,
As swift to and fro in the heavens they go,
   High up overhead in the blue vaulted sky.

Or building their nest and attending their young,
   Until to maturity they have all grown,
When out on the wing from the nest they all spring,
   The house is deserted the birds have all flown.

The summer now wanes and the autumn draws near,
   The nights lengthen out and the days shorter grow,
Migratory birds flock together in herds,
   Our winter they seem to regard as a foe.

And morning by morning the Swallows are seen
   To swarm on the housetops and twitter the while,
The season is late and they now contemplate,
   Escaping the rigours of this sea-girt isle.

They flutter their wings as though testing their strength,
   They twitter a language themselves only know,
Then off they all fly to a more genial sky,
   And over the sea to the summer-land go.

We do not exactly see *when* they depart,
   We miss them and find they no longer are here,
Nor can we discern just the time they return,
   But greatly rejoice when again they are near.

THE RESPONSE.

In reply to an appeal from the Rev. J. Chadburn on behalf of the destitute Poor of East London, Nov. 16th, 1888.

DEAR SIR,

> I beg herewith to send you
>   A trifle from my store,
> And *how* I wish (God only knows)
>   That I could send you more.
>
> My means alas ! are scanty,
>   And only what I earn,
> My friends are poor and have *their* claims.
>   Their claims I may not spurn.
>
> My little ones' well-being,
>   Their Mother's comfort too,
> Depend so much upon myself
>   And what I have to do,
>
> That if my health should fail me
>   (How soon it may God knows),
> Grim poverty might *them* assail,
>   With all its wants and woes.
>
> But though these things may happen,
>   We'll trust the God of all,
> Who numbers e'en our very hairs
>   And notes the sparrow fall.
>
> Your letter of this morning,
>   So forcible and clear,
> Reminds me that though poor myself
>   The *poorer still* are near,
>
> That they are "always with us,"
>   Before our very eyes,
> That we to them a duty owe :
>   Ne'er may we them despise.

Your little houseless wand'rers,
　With shoeless chilblained feet ;
Their faces pale and pinched with want,
　The children of the street.

O how we yearn towards them !
　These little waifs and strays ;
How gladly would we rescue them
　From sin and error's ways !

Men hungry too, and women,
　We much their lot deplore,
As lacking life's necessities,
　They beg from door to door.

We feel we must do something
　To help them in distress,
To brighten up their dreary lives,
　And make their suff'rings less.

So please accept five shillings,
　Which I herewith enclose,
To help to feed your hungry ones
　And buy the needy clothes.

www.ingramcontent.com/pod-product-compliance
Lightning Source LLC
Chambersburg PA
CBHW030539040726
47497CB00008B/2515